Praise for Andrea Dale

"Legendary erotica heavy-hitter."

—über-legendary Violet Blue

"Incredibly erotic."

—Erotica-Readers.com

["The Queen of Christmas" is] "as perfect a blend of sex and humor as rum-spiked eggnog."

—Donna George Storey,
author of *Amorous Woman*

"'Fanning the Flames' by Andrea Dale is perfect for spanking fans and features a delicious twist."

—*Scarlet* magazine UK

["A Few Things to Pick Up on Your Way Home" is] "a sensual trip through humiliation and desire."

—Editor Shanna Germain

["Party Favor" is] "sharp, short, effective."

—Steve Isaak,
Reading & Writing by Pub Light

"'How the Little Mermaid Got Her Tail Back'" (in a sushi restaurant!) is as beguiling as a siren."

—Erin O'Riordan,
Urban Fantasy Writers

Also by Andrea Dale

Novels

A Little Night Music

Novellas

Braceleted
In Her Hands
Kiss on Her List

Collections

Give In
Kiss Me Hello
Naughty in Nature
Quick Licks

KISS
on her
LIST

ANDREA DALE

SOUL'S
ROAD
PRESS

Kiss On Her List
Andrea Dale

Print edition published 2016 by Soul's Road Press

First Edition

ISBN: 978-1-946462-01-5 (trade paperback)

Inquiries should be addressed to
Soul's Road Press
info@soulsroadpress.com
http://www.soulsroadpress.com

Cover image © Alan and Vicena Poulson | Bigstock.com
Logo designed by Designs by Trapdoor

KISS
on her
LIST

chapter one

WHEN YOU GOT to a certain level of fame, Jack Scandal mused, it was really hard to do anything privately.

Oh, you could *have* privacy—you could rent the penthouse of a hotel that catered to the rich and famous, have security posted outside the elevator, the whole shebangy-bangy. But when even a simple birthday party turns into a major event...

It wasn't his birthday, thank goodness. For his birthday, he had been able to sneak away to Aruba with Katerina. That was before the lip-syncing debacle, and losing out on the Grammy, and discovering that Katerina had been with him only because of who he was, and now that he was no longer All That and a Bag of Chips, she was buh-bye, gone.

No, this was Benjy's birthday, and Benjy was his best friend as well as the bass player for Scandalize, and if Benjy wanted his party in the Swiss Alps, then Jack had to stop licking his wounds, drag himself out of his cave, and man up.

In a room full of celebrities, record execs, and—because they couldn't be escaped—the media.

The resort was made up to look like a rustic ski chalet, with exposed natural-wood beams beneath a sharply peaked roof and a stone fireplace big enough to roast a woolly mammoth in. But everything was modern and top of the line, from the caviar that burst brightly on his tongue to the tram system that had ferried them all up here.

Jack nursed a Speyburn and waited for the cake, because once they sang "Happy Birthday," he could bugger out and retreat to his private chalet.

In the meantime, he made nice with the media because if he didn't, within hours TMZ would be claiming he'd become a raging alcoholic and was suicidal or something.

Jack Scandal Hits Rock Bottom!

Yeah, well, screw you.

A huge screen on one wall showed videos from Benjy's favorite band, some grating punk group out of Norway. Thankfully the sound was kept to a level that allowed conversation, because that music was one of the things Jack and Benjy disagreed on.

Currently, they also disagreed on the way out of Jack's funk, because Benjy had wandered over earlier, stood with him in respectful silence for a moment, and finally said, "Bro. You know what you need? You need to get laid. Get KatFight right outta your system."

Maybe Benjy was right. Get back on the proverbial horse. Jack scanned the room. At six-two, he was tall enough to see over most of the hundred or so people milling about.

There were some seriously beautiful women here. Problem was, most of them would rather not be seen with him right now.

He clearly hadn't thought it through when he'd picked the stage name *Scandal* ten years ago. Back then, at the cocky age of nineteen, he'd thought it sounded more sexy and rock-and-roll than Scanlan.

It was as if he'd just *handed* headlines to the paparazzi. Way to think that one through.

Meanwhile, even if someone was interested right now, no other woman had really interested *him* since Katerina.

Until he spotted *her*.

Jack perked up so fast, he felt like his childhood dog, Spitfire, when the leash came out. On the inside.

Somehow, in a room full of the elitely gorgeous, she managed to stand out.

She wore an emerald green sheath dress that hugged her body like a Formula One car on a road circuit—she had curves, unlike the supermodels, and those curves looked natural, even unfashionably so. The dress glittered with sequins, but had a simple cut: sleeveless, with a deep vee neck to show some cleavage, and falling to mid-thigh. Next to some of the scraps of fabric that women called clothes these days, the dress looked positively sexy on her.

He wanted to peel it off her. Slowly. It probably had a zipper at the back, and there was nothing like drawing down a zipper and watching the smooth skin of a woman's back appear, inch by deliberate, glorious inch, until it reached the tantalizing upper curve of her ass.

Her red hair skimmed her jaw in a straight pageboy style, also not fashionable, but it suited her. She had her own style, wore it with self-assurance.

A woman like that knew her own mind, knew what she liked. Especially in bed.

She was standing at the bar, chatting with Meredith Orran, the head of marketing at GWN, Scandalize's record label. The redhead must have felt his gaze on her because she glanced over at him.

Jack felt the air leave his lungs in a rush. He raised his chin, acknowledging her.

Even from across the room, he could see the slow smile spread across her lips. She nodded back.

Then a quartet of white-jacketed waiters, pushing a cart topped with something so tall it blocked his view across the room for a second, crossed in front of him. By the time they passed, the woman was gone.

Jack felt bereft. But a few moments later, a server appeared at his shoulder. "From the lady at the bar," she said, handing him a small glass containing two fingers of a caramel-colored liquid.

He'd finished his first glass of whiskey over the past hour. He took a sip of this one. Toffee, vanilla, and spice. Another Speyburn. Nice.

Then he saw her moving through the crowd to him, matching glass in her hand, and the rest of the room dropped away.

The redhead walked with a confidence few women possessed, because it came with personality, somehow. Any supermodel could walk with authority. There was just no life behind it.

But this woman…

He felt the pressure in his groin, felt his cock nudge up against the fly of his black leather pants.

This woman was something else.

chapter two

AAAAND…CONTACT.

Darby Hayes sensed Jack Scandal, lead singer and guitarist of Scandalize, watching her from across the room, and felt a thrill of anticipation like a lover's hot whisper across her naked flesh.

Not just the anticipation of seducing one of the hottest men in rock and roll. The anticipation of crossing *Rock and Roll* off her list afterwards.

Her best friend and business partner, Jennifer, claimed Darby had made the list because she was bored, and Jennifer, being a whip-smart woman, was probably right. Darby had just never cared to analyze it.

She liked men. She liked sex. She liked a challenge. She liked making lists and crossing items off the list as she accomplished them.

The list was simple, really. The goal was to have hot monkey sex with the following men who were at the top of their careers: football player, baseball player, basketball player, hockey player, race car driver, rock star, country star, movie star, TV star.

She was about halfway through the list, although she considered adding more. She just wasn't sure about the categories yet. Stage actors were tough because a good percentage would be more interested in the men on her list. Jockeys were too short. Fortune 500 CEOs were generally too old. (Not that older men couldn't be sexy as hell. Just…most of the CEOs weren't.)

Now, Jack. She glanced at him, and when she was sure she had his attention, she smiled.

Friendly. A little seductive, but not too overt. *Hi, I see you watching me, and you're hot.*

He raised his chin in greeting, and she nodded. Excellent. Time to get this party started.

"Meredith, I'm so glad we had the chance to talk," she said to the woman she'd been chatting with. If Darby ever wanted to take her company public, she'd definitely try to steal Meredith away from GWN. But right now, she was happy keeping things small. Then she turned to the bartender and said, "Could you please send another glass of Speyburn to Jack Scandal? One for me as well."

The young man poured the drinks and handed one to her and one to a server with instructions. Darby smiled, thanked him, and slid a hundred-dollar bill across the bar to him because there was no tip jar. The drinks were free, of course. High-end alcohol flowed like water here.

She didn't make money for the sake of making money. Money was a tool to allow you to do the things you really wanted to do. The ostentation of this resort and the party itself were fun, but she wouldn't have spent it on herself. She lived a fairly low-key life, all things considered.

However, when she needed ready cash—to charter a last-minute flight to Switzerland, and grease the right palms to get an invitation to Benjy Munroe's birthday party, and have the right dress and shoes and lingerie delivered—it was available.

She headed across the room. Jack Scandal had made the first move, expressed interest. She always let the men initiate the encounter. If they weren't interested, neither was she.

She didn't stalk them. She didn't coerce them, she didn't trick them, and she certainly didn't force them.

She offered them something they might want: a night of sex with a willing, interested, attractive woman.

Okay, maybe she stalked them a little, for two good reasons: One, to ensure her own safety. She had the ability to drill pretty damn deep into their private lives, and if she found anything dangerous, especially kinky, or seriously illegal in their lives, they got knocked right off the short list for the category.

And two, she made damn sure they weren't in a relationship already. She would never, ever try to sleep with a man in a committed relationship. She was not that kind of girl. She had rules, and that was an unbreakable one.

Bonus points, however, if they'd just been through a breakup. That way, maybe she could help mend their broken heart and put the confident spring back in their step, so to speak.

Sexual healing, as the song went.

Goodness knew Jack Scandal needed it.

Good thing she was the right woman for the job.

Heat pooled in her belly, and she felt herself growing slick as she walked towards him. This part was like a dance—a tango. Give and take. Escalate a little each time. Ratchet up the interest, the desire.

This part was almost more fun than the sex, because it still wasn't a done deal.

Almost, but not quite. Who was she kidding? The sex really was the best part.

There was something about Jack Scandal that resonated with her. All of the men she picked were her type in some form or another, but it was as if he'd been created for her.

Long, thick black hair that flowed with his movements. Dark blue eyes, intense as fuck. Perfectly cultivated stubble highlighting a firm jaw and cheekbones that could cut glass. And oh, that body. Long-legged and lean, with biceps she wanted to gnaw on and the best ass in rock and roll in those tight black leather pants.

"Thank you for the drink," he said, and his smoky voice, with just the hint of a rasp, made her want to purr and rub herself against him like a cat.

"Thank you for introducing me to Speyburn," she said, lifting her own drink.

It wasn't a lie. He didn't need to know she didn't learn what he was drinking from the bartender. She never tried to turn herself into some desperate attempt at a perfect woman for each man, but a few mutual interests helped with the seduction.

She liked the Speyburn very much, in fact.

"Darby Hayes, by the way."

"Jack Scandal."

He took her outstretched hand, and the callouses on his fingertips from guitar playing rasped gently against her skin. She imagined those fingers on her breasts, and the roughness of his stubble against the sensitive flesh of her inner thighs…

Goodness. She'd never gotten this excited, this fast before. All of the men she chose were sexy. Most rockers were sexy on stage, but Jack Scandal brought it with him everywhere, it seemed. He wasn't sexy—he was sex personified. It was all she could do to not start fanning herself.

"Yes, I know," she said. "I promise not to go all fan-girl on you, but I am a Scandalist." It was the politest word the band's fans called themselves.

"And here I thought you might be in the industry," he said. His eyes never left hers, but she knew he already had the look of her painted in his mind.

She laughed. "Goodness, no. I own a software company. I'm here because of a friend of a friend." Sort of true.

"What do you think of the party?"

"Well…" She shrugged one shoulder, let the dangling emerald earrings she wore twist and shimmer. "Would it be awful if I said there are other things I'd rather be doing?"

"Not at all." He sipped his drink, letting it linger on his tongue before swallowing. The motion fascinated her somehow. "Tell me…what would you rather be doing?"

She pretended to think about it, and leaned a little closer to confide in him. He smelled like whiskey and leather and something else she couldn't quite define. Scandal. The good kind.

"It's beautiful outside, the full moon on the snow turning everything this astonishing shade of blue I've never seen anywhere else," she said. "So I'd go for a walk. Then to warm up, I'd relax in the hot tub, and maybe curl up on the sofa with a glass of champagne."

Now he leaned in, dipping his head down towards her, an intimate move that brought them into their own private sphere, and lowered his voice, his words only for her.

"Ah, but would you be doing those things alone?"

She felt a jolt of excited energy. The heat in her belly spiraled out, down.

She had him.

"Since you brought it up…"

chapter three

JACK FOUND IT incredibly enticing that Darby Hayes wasn't throwing herself at him. An obviously willing woman could be too easy. She was giving him the thrill of the chase, making him work for it a little bit.

She understood the game, the give-and-take. It was refreshing.

It was undeniably arousing.

He'd given her an opening. He couldn't wait to see how she took it, escalated it, tossed it back to him.

She wore some kind of musky scent that filled his senses, or maybe it was just her scent, but whichever it was, he didn't want to draw back and stop being surrounded by it. Her dangling earrings caught in the light, which drew his gaze to the line of her throat, the shadow of her collarbone, and he wanted to taste her there.

Taste her everywhere, and hear her words turn into moans.

"Since you brought it up…" she began, a wicked glint in her grey-green eyes.

"*Jack-eee!*" Benjy's wail—familiar to anyone who'd ever attended a Scandalize concert—pierced the room. "Caaaaaake!"

After music, sugar was Benjy's favorite thing. Even women came in third…at least sometimes.

"I'm sorry," he said to Darby, and he truly was. "I have to be a part of this."

She smiled, shook her head once, and extended her hand to the low stage where Benjy stood next to an enormous cake topped with what looked to be a life-sized red guitar made out of marzipan. "Do your thing," she said. "I'll be waiting."

She made it sound like a promise. A promise of more to come.

(With any luck, both of them. Repeatedly. He wanted to see the look in those big smoky eyes of hers when…)

Well, hell. There was no way he could calm himself before he got to the stage with Benjy and the rest of the band. Oh well…if a photographer got a shot of him with his leather pants bulging, there wasn't much disparaging they could say about it, could they?

He bounded up onto the stage. A few people actually cheered. Those people were, no doubt, very drunk.

The cake wasn't quite big enough for a naked woman to jump out of, unless the woman was a midget, and given that Jack had been in charge of such details (the cake, not strippers), he knew they were safe.

He grabbed his acoustic guitar, strummed a few notes, and got "Happy Birthday" going, putting a few flourishes on it just because. *Print this, you fuckers: His voice sounded fine when he sang "Happy Birthday."*

While the staff cut the cake and distributed the plates, the band pulled him into a few more impromptu Scandalize songs, a cappella except for the guitar (and Tony kept the beat on a table, because he was never without sticks).

All the while, he kept watching Darby.

What killed it was when she took a bite of cake and got some frosting at the corner of her mouth. With her pinky, she caught it and drew it to her mouth. The tip of her tongue peeked out just far enough to catch the buttercream.

All the while, she watched him.

A lesser woman would have full-on sucked her own finger, which bordered on crass. This was much more seductive. The action slammed straight into his groin.

Enough.

He put the guitar in its case, jumped down, strode over to her. "It is a beautiful night," he agreed, "but I'm not exactly in the mood for walking."

"You're reading my mind," she said.

chapter four

DARBY HAD BEEN honest when she said she'd never seen such a breathtaking shade of blue like the Alpine snow in the moonlight.

Unfortunately, that sight was gone, because now clouds obscured the moon and snow fell in huge, fluffy flakes. The Range Rover driver deftly navigated the road up to the private chalets. He carried Jack's guitar case in, asked if there was anything else he could do for them, and when the answer was no, left.

Darby's hands shook just the tiniest bit with lust as she let Jack ease her out of her coat.

The chalet was in the same style as the lodge. A spacious, two-story living room with overstuffed brown leather furniture draped in fuzzy, cream-colored blankets. Electronics clearly hidden behind wooden panels painted with a mountain scene. A river-rock fireplace, the fire lit and welcoming, and champagne chilling in a silver urn on the rustic-inspired coffee table. A spiral staircase led up to a balcony overlooking the living room, probably leading to the bedroom.

The place smelled like pine and wood smoke. Masculine.

She slipped out of her boots and slid her feet back into her heels. She liked the way they shaped her legs (and most men did, too), plus they brought her closer to Jack's height.

Better for kissing. Better when he bent her over the back of that sofa, if that's how things went.

She walked over to the window, looked out at the falling snow. She heard the pop of the champagne cork, and watched in the window reflection as Jack poured a glass and walked to her. A moment later, she felt him behind her. His arm reached around and she accepted the flute. Took a sip and savored the crispness, the bubbles.

Jack was standing so close, she could feel the heat of him on her back. She shifted, moving back a fraction of a step. He took the hint and moved forward, his arm now encircling her waist, gently urging her against him.

Her breath caught. His cock rested against her tailbone, hard, insistent. It woke every nerve in her body, faster than she expected. She needed him soon.

"Beautiful view," he murmured, and she knew he wasn't talking about the snow. With his free hand—he'd never poured himself champagne—he eased aside her hair and bent to press his lips against the curve where her neck met her shoulder.

The touch turned her veins to liquid fire. He kissed her there, unhurried, as if learning her taste and savoring it. She couldn't stop the sigh that escaped her, and she moved her hips against the hard length of him, just a little, letting him know how he affected her. In response, he caught his breath.

Enough. She turned, raising her arms so she could put them around his neck. The press of his cock against her groin was maddening, and she wished she could snap her fingers and make their clothes dissolve.

She wished that, but she ached for the foreplay, the seduction, just as much.

She wasn't sure who groaned just before their lips met.

This kiss made her legs weak. Slow at first, exploring, his tongue meeting hers in the age-old dance that was so new to them. But a moment later, as if by mutual agreement, the kiss deepened. She drank him in, devouring, nipping at his lower lip, letting him know he didn't need to treat her with kid gloves.

Without breaking the kiss, he plucked the glass out of her hand and set it somewhere. Then his hands went beneath her ass and he picked her up. Instinctively she wrapped her legs around his waist. The motion hiked up her dress, and now the only barriers between them were her silk panties, his leather trousers, and whatever he might or might not be wearing beneath them.

He carried her without a problem over behind the sofa she'd been contemplating earlier, settling her on the back of it. She left her legs clamped around him, pulling him as close as she could. The pressure of his hardness against her clit was maddening, and she rocked her hips, wanting, needing more.

He made a noise low in his throat and took her face in his hands, kissing her even harder, taking occasional forays to nip at her earlobes, her neck.

Then she felt a hand at her back. He found the zipper of her dress, tugged at it. Some men would have yanked it open. He drew it down slowly, stopping occasionally to run his fingers across the skin he'd revealed.

Here, she thought, was a man who knew how to savor the moment. Who knew what he wanted.

Finally, when it was all the way down, he slid the dress off one shoulder, then the other. Between the two of them, they got the dress off her arms, down to her waist.

She watched his nostrils flare as he took in her bra, black lace and silk and ribbons against her pale skin, and the way her nipples, hard and eager, pressed against the flimsy fabric. Then he put those big, capable hands of his on her ribcage and ran his thumbs across the peaks of sensitive flesh.

She jolted as delicious lightning shot through her, a sharp tug she felt all the way to her clit. He chuckled and did it again. She arched her back, asking for more. He caught her gaze and held it, and she looked back as he continued.

Yes. This. I want this.

His callouses rasped against the silk, and now even the silk was too much of a barrier...

He pulled away, and she gulped for air, dizzy from the lack of it, and from desire.

"Upstairs," was all he said.

"Yes," she answered simply.

He probably would have carried her there if he could, but the spiral staircase didn't lend itself to that.

He stepped back, and she stood on shaking legs, letting her dress drop to the floor. She kicked off her shoes, too, because no matter how good they looked, she wasn't confident she could make it up the stairs in them.

He held out his hand, and she took it, but paused. "Condoms?" She had some in her purse, of course. She never hacked into their medical records.

"Got 'em," he said.

Just off the balcony, a pair of double doors opened onto the bedroom. Darby didn't have much time—or interest—in anything but the massive bed with more pillow and bolsters than God. Jack thumbed some switches, and a few lights came on around the room.

She turned and watched as he stripped off his shirt, then she stepped forward so she could splay her hands across his chest, feel the play of muscles and the skin and the dusting of dark hair.

Their hands reached the fly of his leather pants at the same time, and he pulled back, letting her do the honors.

Nothing on beneath. Perfect. His cock, freed, was also perfect. She wrapped her hand around it, and he sucked in a breath. "Careful," he murmured. A warning that he was as close as she was. She smiled, took a step backwards, and of course he followed, stepping out of his pants. When the backs of her knees hit the bed, she sat, then slid her way up to half-sit, half-lie against the pillows.

He was there a second later, straddling her legs, reaching for the front clasp of her bra. She moaned in anticipation even before he touched her. Then his mouth and hands were on her, teasing her sensitive nipples with gently grazing teeth and massaging fingers.

She turned the moan into a "More," unable to think beyond that word, that need. Her hips moved of their own volition; she writhed as he gave her just the amount of extra roughness she craved.

She reached for his cock again, unable to do more than encircle it with her fingers, rub her thumb through the wetness at the tip. She wanted to taste him.

Later. Now she wanted…she wanted…

He shifted on the bed, and she raised her hips to allow him to slide her panties off. They were ruined anyway.

He didn't need to nudge her thighs apart. He knelt, nipped playfully on her inner thigh, and then thank you dear lord *finally* touched her.

He drew his callous-roughened fingers in lazy circles around her clit until she thought she'd scream from need. She wasn't the type to beg, but that rule was about be broken if only he would—

He switched up the motion, more direct. Her world narrowed to the need spiraling tighter, higher… Her legs trembled, her belly tensed, her fingers fisted in the bedspread.

"So beautiful," he said hoarsely. "Want to watch you… watch you come for me."

And with that, she convulsed. All the desire, the tension, the build-up came down to this one moment of exquisite release.

Somehow he kept his hands on her, rode with her as she arched off the bed. She fell back, barely had time to draw in a breath before his mouth was on her, urging her up, up, up again. That stubble rasped against her thighs, and his tongue, oh sweet mercy that tongue… She shuddered through a second orgasm that hit her faster than she'd experienced before.

She was his instrument, she thought drunkenly, and he played her with amazing expertise. He drew desire out of her like he did a melody from his guitar strings.

She watched, eyes half-lidded, as he rolled the condom onto that impressive cock of his. Her inner walls twitched, half after-spasm, half anticipation. He was going to feel glorious inside her.

He urged her up, over, onto her knees. Oh, yes, this was going to be glorious indeed.

"Hold on," he said.

"Just the words I like to hear," she purred, grabbing the headboard.

He slid into her the way he'd kissed her: savoring the moment. She glanced over her shoulder. His head was thrown back, cords of his throat tensed, black hair spilling down his back.

Teasing, toying, she thrust back just a tiny bit to take the rest of him in. His head rocked forward, eyes snapping open. She winked.

That was all the go-ahead he needed. He pulled out, snapped his lean hips, thrust hard. It took them a moment to find their rhythm, but when they did, it was just as glorious as she'd anticipated. The hard length and breadth of him, moving, filling, urging her back up again. His hands came around her, onto her breasts, finding her nipples again, adding to her pleasure.

Another orgasm rolled through her; slow build, slow release, like the long inexorable roll of an ocean wave, rising and crashing. The moan that escaped her throat followed the same long, slow measure.

"Jesus, Darby, I felt—feel…" Jack's word's dissolved into a groan. He grabbed her hips, and his thrusts went erratic, staccato, as he came.

He leaned over her, hands on the headboard outside of hers, his chest to her back, sucking in air.

"Jack, that was…wow." She shook her head, at a loss for words.

Then a squeak of surprise escaped her, because he flipped her over onto her back again.

"Encore?" he suggested, and before she could remember how to form words, he was between her legs again, his tongue flicking against her clit. At the same time, he slid three of his amazing fingers inside her. She was almost too sensitive, but she could tell immediately, as the desire built, that her body had one more sweet orgasm left in it.

He crooked those fingers in a "come here" motion, and oh, she did. This one was sudden, slamming into her like a tidal wave, knocking the breath out of her lungs.

She sprawled on the pillows, arms flung out, unable to move. He flopped down next to her on his back, and half gasped, half laughed.

"Happy birthday to me," he said finally.

She rolled onto her side. "No," she said. "It's not really." If she had half a brain cell left, she'd be able to remember his birthday. A basic piece of information. Sweet lord, what had he done to her?

"No, it's not, but it feels like my birthday and Christmas and every other major holiday wrapped into one," he said. The grin on his face made him look almost vulnerable. He rolled onto his side, facing her, and touched her face. "You're incredible."

"I'd say you had a lot to do with it, too," she said.

He got up to dispose of the condom. She watched him walked to the bathroom, committing that fine, naked ass to memory. He returned with two glasses of water.

After that workout, she needed it.

"Do you need anything else?" he asked. "Should I grab the champagne? Food?"

"I'm fine," she said. She smiled. "More than fine."

He came back to the bed, pulled the chenille blanket at the foot of it halfway over them, draped an arm over her. He gently cupped her breast.

"Give me a few minutes to recharge," he said. "I'm thinking Round Two is going to be even more spectacular."

"Mmm," she said. He took it as she intended him to, as post-sex hazy agreement.

That wasn't what she meant.

There wasn't going to be a Round Two. There never was. "Recharging" meant a nap, she knew. And she never *slept* with the men on her list.

As his breathing slowed, indicating just that, she realized she'd briefly forgotten about the list. Usually she made a mental checkmark before the man entered her, but she'd been so overcome, so needy and desperate, that everything else had fled her mind, leaving nothing but the moment and passion and the sensations.

She waited a few more minutes, then eased herself out from under his arm. Her underwear wasn't in plain sight, so she left it. She padded down the spiral staircase and used the lower level bathroom so she didn't wake him, then found her dress. Shimmied into it and zipped it back up, remembering with satisfaction the measured way he'd unzipped it, savoring the experience.

Boots and coat, shoes and purse in hand. She braced herself for the cold and opened the front door of the chalet.

And stopped, aghast.

The snow was two, two-and-a-half feet high, piled right up against the door—and still coming down hard.

From behind her, Jack said, "That doesn't look good."

She turned. He leaned against the balcony rail in all his hot, lean, naked glory. He grinned.

"Looks like we're stuck with each other for awhile."

chapter five

JACK HAD BEEN only half-asleep when Darby slid out from under his arm. He assumed she'd been headed to the bathroom, and dozed again, until he resurfaced and realized he didn't hear any bathroom noise.

That's when he came out and saw her trying to leave.

Her actions stung, but didn't entirely surprise him. Although he thought he'd made it clear he hoped she'd stay, some women did prefer their one-night stands to be just that.

He was disappointed; he'd thought Darby was better than that, thought she wasn't just a groupie looking to score. His judgment must be screwed up, big time. He'd been looking forward to Round Two, and maybe Three, and breakfast somewhere in there, and then…

He hadn't really thought past that, but he definitely wanted more. And maybe now he'd get his chance. Even if she preferred the wham-whack-thank-you-Jack, she couldn't be completely averse to spending a little more time together.

He *knew* she'd enjoyed herself. There was no way she could have faked her reactions. The orgasmic flush that spread across her pale, lightly freckled chest was just as much of a turn-on as those perky breasts tipped with responsive...

Darby looked back outside, back at him, and again, as if she couldn't believe what she saw. Even from up here, he could see her eyes were wide, and it looked as though she'd gone pale.

"Darby?" He hurried down the stairs. "Are you okay?"

Cold air poured in through the open door, and snow was starting to drift in as well. He reached around her and pushed the door shut, then put an arm around her. Her grey-green eyes were still wide, and he wondered if she was having some kind of medical issue. Low blood sugar? Did that put someone into shock? As if he knew what shock looked like.

"Are you okay?" he repeated.

chapter six

OH GOD, HE thought she was having a medical issue. Maybe this *was* a panic attack; she didn't know. But she had to pull herself together before he called the Swiss version of 911 and an Airflight medical helicopter came.

"I'm fine," she said, and forced a little laugh, trying to brush off his concern. "I've just never seen that much snow before. Are we stuck until spring?" Good plan. Make a joke.

Her brain raced. This wasn't according to plan. This could screw up her whole system. She'd already checked him off her list, dammit.

He chuckled. "No, just until the snow stops and the plows can come through, I would think. Or maybe they can get snowmobiles through in the morning. Meanwhile…are you hungry?"

"No. Yes. Maybe?" God, she was really rattled.

"Good, because I'm starved. But first things, first." He helped her out of her coat for the second time that night (so wrong), then strode across the living room to the bathroom, unselfconscious of his nudity.

He was really beautiful. She didn't usually apply that word to a man, but *whuf*.

He re-emerged with two fluffy white robes and handed her one. "Don't want to catch a cold," he said. "I've got to protect my voice."

He glanced at her when he said the words, as if gauging her reaction. She pretended not to noticed, and thanked him as she took the robe. She knew about the lip-syncing debacle: it was one of the reasons she'd chosen him, because he'd gone through a rough patch and probably needed a boost. Clearly he was still uncomfortable about the situation.

"Food sounds great," she said. She needed to regroup, and she *was* hungry.

Feeling strangely self-conscious—an emotion she wasn't used to— she slipped into the bathroom and shimmed out of her dress, then belted the robe firmly around her. The dress was gorgeous, but didn't fit quite right without a bra, and overall wasn't comfortable for lounging. Not that she was going to be lounging. Whatever.

She didn't know what to think.

The other end of the open-plan room had a dining table for eight, and beyond that was a full kitchen, a butcher-block counter separating the cabinets and appliances from the rest of the room. Jack was peering into the open fridge. It was stuffed with food.

"My God, were you planning to host a party?" she asked.

"The resort stocks a variety of food, including any special requests, and provides a personal chef on call," he said. "But I don't think that's going to happen right now. Let's see…" He pulled out several different kinds of cheeses, grapes, strawberries. Where the resort had obtained fresh strawberries at this time of year, Darby couldn't fathom. She found crackers and crisp bread and plates in a cabinet, knives in another.

He added charcuterie, olives, cherry tomatoes to the pile on the counter, then rummaged around until he found a large tray. He piled everything on the tray and took it to the living room, setting it on the coffee table. He poked at the fire, which had died down some, and added a log before settling on the floor and pouring champagne for them both.

She wasn't much of a floor-sitter, but desperate times, and all that. Truth was, she wasn't quite sure how to act. The seduction was over.

Well, except for the fact that she wanted to find out how many creative ways they could use the food. She already had a mental list.

She tried not to think about that. Her body had other ideas.

She did feel a bit better after she'd had a few bites of food. "I'll say this for the Swiss: along with their spectacular mountains, they do know their cheeses. This is marvelous." She pointed to the smooth, blue-veined Roquefort.

"If we can get the chef in, I'll have him make fondue with the local gruyere," Jack said. "Amazing stuff."

Before Darby could process the idea of staying with him that long, he added, "I'm sorry, I forgot to ask if you had any food issues. If you're lactose intolerant, this wasn't the best choice."

"No, this is wonderful," she said. "No food issues."

"If we're snowed in for more than a day, are there any medications you'll need?"

"No worries there," she said, surprised that he'd even think of it. She glanced nervously at the window, but the lights inside reflected the room back to them. Was it still snowing? "Do you think we'll be stuck for that long?"

"A day or two is not that long, unless you hate the person you're with or there's something else bothering you. And it seems like there's something bothering you." He cocked his head. "Not used to one-night stands?"

She choked on a laugh. If he only knew. She shook her head. "Married?"

That chased away the humor. "Absolutely not."

"Well, you clearly didn't have a recorder on you, so you're probably not a reporter looking for dirt."

She'd never considered that. How awful that it was something he had to worry about. She was on alert for corporate espionage in her own world, people trying to get an upper hand in technology, but it hadn't occurred to her that paparazzi would go to those kinds of length for a story.

"Has that really happened?" she asked.

He drank champagne. "Thankfully, no. But you know how it is: you get to a certain level, and a lot of people just want things from you. Katerina apparently did."

"Your girlfriend." Darby knew what the tabloid sites had said.

"She was sympathetic at first, but when things didn't blow over, and then when we didn't get the Grammy, she decided my bad fortune looked bad for her. She didn't want the negative publicity to be directed at her." He leaned back against the sofa. The firelight threw his stubbled jaw into shadows and lines. His hair was still damp at the ends from their energetic sex.

"What really happened, that night at the show?" Darby asked.

"It was the one and only time I've ever used a recording," he said. "There have been a few shows when I was recovering from a cold or something, and Benjy or Shane had to pick up some of the vocals, but this time, I had full-blown laryngitis."

There had been some sort of glitch in the recording during the show, she remembered reading, making it clear he wasn't performing live. The media had had a field day. In the music world, lip-syncing was about akin to marrying your cousin: you knew some people did it, but not anyone you'd respect.

And Jack and Scandalize had been respected in the field. They wouldn't've been up for Best Song at the Grammys otherwise.

"Why didn't you cancel the show?"

"Stupid, I know. If it had been a regular show, we could've issued refunds or rescheduled. A few fans would've been pissed off, but... This was a charity gig, and it was important to me."

Raising money to fund music programs at underprivileged schools, buying instruments and hiring teachers, she remembered.

Funny. She wasn't used to remembering details about the men on her list after the fact.

"But enough about that," he said. He broke off a small bunch of deep purple grapes. "Darby Hayes. Owns a software company. Has killer legs. Amazing in bed. What else? Where do you live?"

She hesitated. That veered a little too close to "I'd like to see you again" territory.

"I'm not going to stalk you," he said. "I'm just… Look, we're going to be here a while. We can't just have sex all the time."

"We're not having sex right now. We're eating." She felt the panic rise in her again and fought to tamp it down. She didn't want to have sex with him again.

Hell, yes, she did. Who was she trying to kid? Every cell in her body yearned for him. She'd been thoroughly sated, but that was before. This was now. Her nipples grew hard beneath her robe, her groin heavy. She wanted to kiss him again. She wanted to taste his cock, feel the weight of it in her mouth, hear the noises he'd make as she pleasured him.

Her body didn't give a flying fuck about the list right now.

"We could be having sex right now," Jack said, his voice low and sexy, "but as you pointed out, we're eating. So why not talk?"

What violated the rules more: Talking or sex? Sex, she decided. She'd done more talking with some of the other men on her list before sex.

And there was something about Jack that intrigued her.

"You're right," she said. "Sorry. Bay Area."

"Makes sense if you own a software company. I'm in LA, but that's probably on my Wikipedia page. Where are you from?"

"All over. Military brat," she explained. "Your parents are British?"

"Mum's Welsh, Dad's English. But I was born and raised in LA. Childhood pet?"

"Didn't have one. All the moving around. You?"

"Jack Russell Terrier named Spitfire." She raised an eyebrow and he continued, "I was really into World War II movies for a year. And no, it's not my answer to the security question on any website."

She laughed. The champagne was smoothing away the jagged edges of her anxiety, and the food was clearly helping her gain her equilibrium, too.

"Okay, my turn," she said. "When did you first pick up a guitar?"

He leaned back against the sofa, spreading his arms along the cushions. The movement tugged open the vee of his bathrobe, exposing more of his hair-dusted chest.

She wanted to run her hands along his skin again. Find out if he liked his nipples played with. Kiss down, untie the sash at his waist, and…

"I've never told anyone this before," he said, "but my first instrument was a ukulele."

Hard-rocking, hip-thrusting, wall-of-sound-and-sex Jack Scandal played the ukulele? She tried, but she couldn't picture it. Not for a hot second.

Her expression must have revealed what she was thinking, because he laughed. "I was four," he said. "A friend of my parents brought it home from Hawaii, and I was fascinated by it. I got my first guitar when I was eight, and in between I also learned piano. Outside of my family, you're the only one who knows, so if this leaks to the media, I know who to blame."

"Your mother?" she asked, blinking her eyes innocently, and they both laughed.

They'd finished eating, and she started to gather up the remains of the food. She wasn't a germaphobe, but she liked things tidy. In their place.

"I've confessed my deep, dark secret; now it's your turn," he said.

Tell him about the list? Not in a million years. The only other person who knew about the list was Jennifer, and she'd take that knowledge to her grave.

He was waiting for her answer. Halfway to the kitchen, she paused, looked over her shoulder coyly, and said, "I'm not wearing any underwear."

She thought he'd laugh, but the flare of desire that flashed in his intense blue eyes floored her.

"I know," he said, in that low growl she'd come to recognize. It triggered a lightning bolt of lust in her, a visceral, Pavlovian response of need. "Your panties are on my pillow. They smell like you."

Breathe. Remember to breathe.

She set the tray on the kitchen island, but instead of putting the food in the fridge and the dishes in the dishwasher, she turned back. The draw of desire, the thread of erotic tension stretching between them, was too strong.

After he'd helped her load the tray, he'd gotten up and added another log to the fire. Now he stood, watching her come back to him.

She'd already told herself that sex a second time would violate the rules. Even then, she suspected she'd known it wouldn't matter.

She craved Jack Scandal's mouth on hers like a drowning woman craved air.

And if she was going to break her own rules, she'd do it on her own damn terms.

chapter seven

SHE WAS HALFWAY back across the room when she unbelted her robe and let it fall to the floor. Jack's cock surged impossibly harder.

Something about Darby affected him in a way no other woman had. He'd wanted other women. Desired them. Loved them, even.

But Darby...he felt as though he'd shatter if he couldn't have her.

Then her body was against him and her lips on his. The intensity of the kiss rocked him back a step. He could tell almost immediately that this wasn't going to be another seduction, another exploration. This time, it was about need and greed and near-desperation.

He wanted to be lost in her, in the feel and taste and smell of her. Consume her and be consumed. Before it had been a slow, building burn. This was a match on gasoline, an immediate conflagration.

She tangled her fingers in his hair, yanked his head down so she could get more of him. He locked his arms around her, dragging her close. Lips, tongue, teeth. He wasn't sure if he devoured her or the other way around. Her wanton, unself-conscious desire made his groin ache, made his cock throb.

When she wedged her hands between their bodies, he released his grip on her so that she could get to the sash of his robe. He needed to be naked, too, feel her body against his.

His cock pressed against her soft belly, her hard nipples pressed against his chest.

"Want you," Darby panted between kisses. "Need you."

"Yes. God yes."

She glanced around, put her hands on his torso to shift his stance, gave a push. He fell backwards into a huge, over-stuffed chair.

Darby sank to her knees, and the last thing he saw was a truly wicked, pleased smile before she lowered her head and took him into her mouth.

Sweet mercy. Every muscle in his body tensed as the world centered on his cock and the feel of Darby's hot, luscious mouth around it.

Some women approached a blow job with enthusiasm, but it was clear their focus was solely on the man's pleasure. Darby was one of those rare creatures who seemed to derive as much from the experience as he did. She tasted him as if she couldn't get enough, stroked his balls with reverence and purpose. When she moaned, he felt the vibrations through his entire body.

She wrapped her fingers around him, mouth and hand stroking the rock-hard length of him, alternating between a tight grip and a loose one, with the occasional twist of her wrist that left him unable to form thoughts. She kept him on edge, ratcheting him up a notch at a time, not enough to come, but close, oh, so close.

As much as he needed more, he thought he could die like this, feeling this, her exquisite touch.

He wanted to make her feel as good as she made him feel. Wanted to hear her cry out again, helpless to the sensations coursing through her body.

With effort, he slid his hands from her shoulders to her face, breaking her rhythm. She made a mew of disappointment that almost tipped him over the edge, and pulled away.

She looked drugged with lust, her eyes glazed, her lips swollen, her hair a tousled mess.

"Want to come inside you," he managed to say.

She rose to her feet in one graceful motion—how she could stand, much less walk, was a miracle to him—and grabbed her purse from the coat rack by the front door. A moment later she was back, condom in hand, already ripping the foil.

The chair was wide enough that she could straddle him, knees on either side of his thighs. She sat back so she could roll the condom down his shaft. She couldn't resist another squeeze, down from the head to the base, and his hips twitched.

A smile twitched her lips in response. She knew what she did to him, and liked it, and that made all the difference.

She braced herself on the back of the chair, hands on either side of his head. Her breasts were temptingly close to his face, and he cupped them in his hands, worshipped them as she'd worshipped his cock. Soft skin, hard nipples…he could touch her forever. She whimpered above him, grinding herself against him, his sheathed cock slipping in her wetness.

She shifted, reached between them, guided him inside.

"So good," she whispered, her breath hot against his ear, when she sank down the full length of him. "So hard…filling me up…"

He kept his hands on her breasts, tweaking and pinching the way he'd learned she liked, letting her do the work. But it wasn't work when it drove them both to the edge. She caught her lower lip in her teeth as she moved up and down, giving a little grind at the bottom. It stabbed him with desire every time.

He needed to come, but he wanted to wait until she'd had her pleasure. Thankfully he didn't have long to wait. Suddenly she cried out, rocking back and forth on him, and he could feel every pulse of her orgasm, gripping his cock.

It was enough for him. It was too much for him. His balls contracted, his thighs tensed, and his world exploded. He drove up into her with a garbled string of sounds that may or may not have included words, and thought, just for a second, that he might have blacked out.

She collapsed against him, and for a moment neither of them could do anything but gasp for air.

He shifted to one side, giving her space next to him. She fell into it, one leg draped across his thighs, one arm across his chest, her head next to his on the cushion. Her chest was flushed and glistening with perspiration.

"Round Two," he said. "More spectacular?"

"Jury's still out," she mumbled, her eyes closed. "Hard to rate spectacular on a scale."

She was spectacular, he thought, and all he wanted right now was to somehow make it upstairs to the bed and then sleep with her wrapped around him, breathing in the scent of two of them combined.

chapter eight

WHEN DARBY WOKE, it was daylight.

And she was alone.

It took her a moment to process that she wasn't in any hotel room, she was in Jack Scandal's chalet. She patted his side of the bed. Still warm; he hadn't been gone long, although she didn't hear any movement in the bathroom.

She stared up at the ceiling. The night before, she hadn't noticed the skylights. The steeply pitched roof kept the snow from accumulating, but the sky was still a flat grey layer of clouds, and a few snowflakes still drifted down.

The worst of the storm might have passed, but it wasn't over yet. It was even possible there'd be another round.

Kind of like her night with Jack.

She pulled one of the many extra pillows over her face and moaned into it. This was all going so very, very wrong.

(So very, very well, her body contradicted. Her thighs ached from last night's energetic workout, and her core was sore. But in a good way. In an "I've been soundly fucked, thank you very much" way. In a "Please, sir, can I have some more?" way.)

No no no.

Last night, Jack had clearly known something was off, because he had offered her a guest room. She surprised herself when she declined. Okay, she hadn't had many brain cells left to rub together, so maybe that's why she made excuses to herself.

Might as well go with the flow; she'd already broken the rules. Maybe not broken. Maybe just a little bent.

The circumstances had been out of her control. The blizzard was act of God. Her plans had been forced to change. She didn't like to admit that, but she couldn't really argue it.

She could have declined having sex the second time, but he was just too delicious. (And, if she was being honest, declining had nothing to do with it. She could have not instigated it. See above re: Jack being too delicious.)

Even the prospect of falling asleep in his arms had seemed like a good idea at the time.

It wasn't as if she'd never had a longer relationship, as if she'd never slept over. She just never did that with the men on her list. They were separate. Special cases.

Some of those men, she wouldn't have minded having sex with again, but she got over it.

She didn't want to get over having sex with Jack.

But she would.

In the shower, she turned the nozzle to its strongest setting and let the hot water pound on her shoulders, which were also sore. Sex used muscles you never expected would be involved.

Nothing much she could do about her hair except run a comb through it. It wouldn't be as sleek, frame her face as well. And she had a powder and lipstick in her purse downstairs, but it wouldn't make much of a difference.

Well, maybe Jack would be less impressed with the Darby who hadn't dropped major bills in the resort spa for hair and makeup. That would make her exit easier.

He'd left clothes for her on the bed: a pair of lounging pants that, although being heather grey and having a drawstring, couldn't really be called "sweatpants," given that they were cashmere and cost nearly a grand. She had to roll up the legs. In contrast, the T-shirt was for some band she'd never heard of. Maybe one Jack was producing; she remembered reading he did that on the side.

She heard Jack's voice before she hit the stairs. He was singing while he made breakfast. Something she didn't recognize. Was Scandalize working on a new album? That, she hadn't researched.

Strange to know so much about him, and yet so little. The few things he'd revealed last night seemed more important than the raft of facts she'd teased into the light.

The facts were to give her an in with the men on her list. She wasn't sure what to do with the rest of it now that she *was* in.

Jack wore nothing but a pair of faded jeans, slung low on his trim hips and molding to his ass like a lover's caress. He moved around the kitchen like he did on stage, with a feline grace—except on stage, there was an added level of danger, as if he were poised, ready to pounce.

"Morning, or afternoon, or something, Luscious," he said when he saw her. He pulled her against him and kissed her soundly.

"Well, good morning, or afternoon, to you, too," she said when she could speak again. Vocally, that was. Her body had a whole lot to say. Like *yes* and *now* and *please*. "You're making…?"

"Omelets. Well, I'm trying. They usually turn into scrambled eggs. I'm thinking goat cheese, asparagus, and garlic."

She watched him for a moment, then shook her head. "I'll make the coffee."

"Excellent—thank you."

She set to work at the professional grade, black-and-chrome espresso maker and made cappuccino. She almost couldn't watch him work. He seemed to be making it all up as he went along, not measuring, just tossing herbs and spices into the whisked eggs, then pouring the mixture into the pan over the already sautéed garlic and not setting a timer.

"Who taught you to cook?" was the only way she could think to phrase the question.

"My dad." He crumbled the cheese over the eggs. "He said it was to survive his own mother's cooking."

"So you've got the recipe in your head?"

He shrugged. "Just the basic idea. I mean, eggs aren't very hard. Mix them with some milk or cream and seasoning, cook them with whatever's handy. Take them off the heat just before they're done—just a little runny—because they'll keep cooking a bit after you plate them. How about we have some of the cold cuts and fruit with them? There might be some bread for toast somewhere."

Shaking her head, she pulled out the rest of the food, set out silverware and napkins on the island where there was a bar stool on each side of the corner.

"I've never poisoned anyone, if that's what you're worried about," he added. "What about you?" he asked. "Cook or no?"

"I cook," she said, finishing up the coffee. "I just…follow recipes."

"Recipes are a great jumping-off point," he agreed. He tried to flip the omelet, but it broke. Scrambled it was, then. "But following to the letter? What's the fun of that? They're like music: once you understand the rules, you understand how to break them."

"But rules are there for a reason: to make everything run smoothly."

He scooped the scrambled omelet onto two plates. "Things run too smoothly, it's boring. There's no creativity. No magic."

"There's no magic in software design," she said. "The marketing department can be creative all it wants." She tasted the eggs. They were good. Really good. All the tastes exploded on her tongue, complementing each other and making the whole better than the sum of its parts. Like wine and cheese.

She glanced out the window. The snow peeked over the edge of the sill. "Any idea when we'll get out of here?"

"Damn, woman, can't you even finish your breakfast first? What is your rush? Who's waiting at home? Fretting mother? Hungry cat? Surely there's someone you can call to take care of your cat."

"I don't have a cat! I was making conversation. These eggs are really good. Thank you."

"The coffee is superb—thank *you*," he said. "That was better. I did call down to the main lodge. Unless there's an emergency, they're probably not going to be able to get us out until late this afternoon. The snow's a little too deep and powdery for snowmobiles to come through safely, so it's a matter of getting things plowed out."

She blew out a breath. She could make it until then, surely.

Her tablet was down at the main lodge. She could check her email on her phone, and call Jennifer, and see if there was anything on her agenda she could do remotely.

(*Or just have sex with Jack again. And again*, her traitorous body suggested.)

She realized Jack was watching her, a bemused smile on his sensual lips. "What?"

"Just thinking about today," he said. "Something like, foreplay in the hot tub, then some acrobatic sex, then maybe a shower—which might lead to more sex, you never know—and then food, because we'll need to keep our strength up. Or sex and then relax in the hot tub. Could go either way. Have a preference?"

"I…" The moment he'd said *sex*, her brain had gone to mush. Finally she laughed. "I'm not used to having my day not planned out."

"You know what they say: 'If you can spend a perfectly useless afternoon in a perfectly useless manner, you have learned how to live.'"

"You have that memorized."

"Words to live by. Although I'm not calling sex perfectly useless." He wrapped his long, capable, *talented* fingers around his mug and leaned on the butcher block. "You don't agree?"

"I live by the mountain philosophy," she said. "The idea that the mountain in the distance, that's your goal. You have to keep your eye on the mountain. It's a long journey, and everything you do has to be taking you towards the mountain. If you lose sight, get distracted, you'll do something that leads you off the path and takes you farther away from your goal."

"Hm. I can see some validity to that—I believe in going after what you want. But what if you're facing the wrong mountain?"

"What?" That didn't even make sense.

"Things change. People change, circumstances change. What if another mountain is more aligned with what you want? What if that meandering path takes you on an amazing journey you never could have predicted?"

"What if the path is a dead end?" she countered.

He thought for a moment. "Come here," he said. He stood and held out his hand, and because there was no earthly reason to do anything else, she took it. The simple touch still zinged through her. His hand was warm from the coffee, comforting, strong. It felt like being wrapped in his arms when she fell asleep last night, except now she didn't feel sated.

Now even the cashmere drawstring pants felt like far too many clothes.

He sat her on the sofa, then took his acoustic guitar out of its case and sat on the chair on which they'd made energetic love last night. She folded her hands in her lap to keep herself from going over to him and suggesting they repeat the experience by showing him what she'd like to do...

He strummed the guitar, twisted the pegs to tune it, strummed again. His head was bowed, but he didn't seem to be looking at the strings. His eyes were closed; he was listening.

A moment later he began to sing. Nonsense syllables, half under his breath. Then words along with the chords. She realized he was singing about facing a mountain, intent on a goal.

Coming from him, it was beautiful.

Then he paused, hummed, and started again with different chords. The song snippet sounded even better, even to her untrained ear. Before, it had been beautiful. Now it was almost heartbreaking.

He stopped, resting his hand on the strings. "Music is perfectly useless, at least when it comes to goals," he said. "Yes, I wanted to be a working musician, and everything I did was focused on that, including learning my craft. But writing music, playing music, even listening to music…if you don't let go and let the music take you, you'll never find the heart of it. You heard me change the key."

"Yes," she said. "The second one sounded better—felt better." She touched her breastbone. "Here."

"Exactly. I didn't follow any rule there. I followed my gut, my ear. Yes, that's based on years of learning and practice, but in the end it's about emotion and instinct."

He sang again, changing up the lyrics a little, changing chords, picking out a melody. When he stopped again, he was smiling.

"And you were doing exactly what you needed to be doing: listening. Music can be part of a perfectly useless day. It's not for multitasking: it's for stopping and listening and being." He paused, looked down, strummed once, stopped the sound with his palm.

"It's there, and then it's gone, but it lives inside of you forever. But it can still…end."

He set the guitar in its case, came and sat on the sofa next to her, sideways with one arm along the back so he could face her.

"Here's something else I haven't told anybody. Before I played that charity show, my doctor thought my laryngitis might be something else. Something worse. I was waiting to hear the results of a biopsy. But I still wanted to go on—I could still play, even if I couldn't sing."

"Oh my God," Darby said. "Are you…you're all right?"

"Biopsy was negative. Some rest was all I needed in the end. But I was too scared to tell anybody. Not the band, not even Benjy. Not even my parents or Katerina. In fact, I didn't even get the chance to tell her the results were clean before she left. In hindsight, I should've told her everything from the start."

"Would she have stayed?"

He thought. "Probably not. She showed her true colors."

"The press might have been more forgiving if they knew," Darby said.

"Maybe. But it wasn't any of their business—or they might have spun it into a whole frenzy about me losing my voice. I don't want people to come to a show to see how badly I suck." He ran a hand through his hair. "This'll blow over, I hope. The label hasn't dumped us. I just feel bad the fans felt like I've let them down."

He picked up her hand, twined her fingers with his. "But that's not my point. My point is, like music, life shouldn't always follow a direct path. Think about this: if you'd stayed home and worked, facing your mountain, instead of coming to Benjy's birthday party, we never would have met."

But work wasn't the mountain she'd been heading towards then. Her list was another mountain entirely.

And if she deviated off that path—if she stayed with Jack longer than she had to—if she let Jack into her heart…she'd never get back on the path. She'd never finish her list.

She'd *fail*.

He was waiting for her to say something.

"I did some networking at the party," she said, and the words sounded flat even to her. She tried again. "But you're right, just because I'm stuck here for another few hours doesn't derail my goals." She'd bent the rules, but they weren't broken. She wasn't falling for Jack. "I can spend a day doing perfectly useless things."

"She says, defensively." He was grinning.

"Careful, or I'll call you useless."

"Liar." He was moving closer, and her breath came in shorter gasps. Her heart pounded, and her nipples perked up, just from his proximity. "I think you've found me very useful so far."

Like a big cat pouncing, his mouth was suddenly at her ear, teeth grazing her flesh.

"Well," she panted. "Maybe…parts…of you."

He laughed in her ear, husky, sexy, wicked, and full of promise. "Let's find out which parts."

If she'd had the capacity for thought, she would have made a list: Mouth. Tongue. Even the hair that slid across her breasts after he tugged his T-shirt over her head.

Hands. Fingers. They were on the floor, on the sheepskin in front of the fireplace, and he pinned her wrists with one of his hands. Used his other hand, and mouth and tongue and teeth, to tease and tempt and toy. Suckling her nipples. Sliding down between her legs to stroke her clit, like a butterfly whisper at first, then, as she moved restlessly, needing more, he gave that to her.

Still not enough. Her clit, swollen, pulsed at his touch. She moaned, arched her back, pleading.

Then he was between her legs, his mouth on her, those talented fingers sliding inside, working in tandem until her heels scrabbled against the floor as she came, helplessly, over and over again, not realizing until after that he'd long since let go of her wrists.

Then, his cock. Finally. He threaded his fingers through hers, held her hands over her head, but this was an intimate gesture. Some small part of her brain protested—too far, too close, too something—but then he entered her and there was nothing but sensation and clenching around him and another sweet, powerful release.

chapter nine

HE WAS IN the bathroom, disposing of the condom, when the phone rang. Since there was a line in the bathroom, he answered it there.

When he came out, she was curled up on the sofa, wrapped in a blanket. He could just spy a hint of rosy nipple peeking through a gap. She was gazing at the fire. Not doing anything else.

He smiled. Maybe she was taking that useless day thing to heart. Maybe it meant the news wouldn't affect their idyll.

She'd brought glasses of cucumber-mint water from the dispenser in the kitchen, and she handed one to him as he sat next to her.

"The lodge called," he said. "Plows are coming through. We should be cleared out in half an hour or so."

She blinked, as if coming out of a trance. "Oh," she said. "I…should take a quick shower." She started to stand, but he caught her wrist, gently. Tugged her back down.

"Stay," he said simply.

"I can't."

"Then I'll come to San Jose, or wherever you are."

"Jack, no—"

"You can't work twenty-four/seven."

"It's not that…" She looked distressed, almost panicked, her eyes wide like they'd been when she discovered they were snowed in.

"Then why?" he demanded, frustrated. "You haven't given me a reason every time it's come up. What are you hiding?"

He'd thought things were going well. When they talked about music…he thought they'd made some connection.

She stood, paced back and forth. He caught glimpses of skin, the length of her legs, and it was even sexier than when she was naked.

Except now she wore the blanket like armor. A barrier between the two of them.

A barrier between her and her emotions.

"Okay, I'll tell you. But you have to understand…it was never meant to go any further than one night. One really good night. Okay?"

Before he could respond, even processed, she launched into her explanation. She had a list, she explained. Men, top of their fields in the arts and sports. He was, apparently, the rock-and-roll checkmark on her bucket list.

She wasn't all that different from the other groupies, the ones he had taken to avoiding. She had a more elaborate plan, but still.

Finally she ran out of things to say. She stopped in front of the fireplace, watching him, clearly hoping he'd understand, be okay with being a to-do item on her crazy list.

"So, you just used me," he said.

"Did you enjoy it?" she asked.

Oh, how he had. They'd barely finished, and her words made him do a flash review of every position, every orgasm over their time together, and his cock twitched against his thigh. He felt doubly betrayed now.

"I think you know I did," he said.

"Then what. Is. The. Problem?"

"I suppose I thought we had more of a connection than that."

She sat down hard in an easy chair—not the one they'd had sex in, he noted.

"We talked for what—five, ten minutes before we left the party?" she asked. "That's not a lot to base a connection on. Remember, I wasn't even going to spend the night. Are you telling me you've never had a one-night stand?"

"Of course I've had one-night stands. I—"

She held up her hand. "And did any of the women sleep with you solely because you're a rock god?"

"Well, yes, I'm sure some of them did. We never really talked about it." But he knew.

"So why is this different?"

Because…because I want you.

She'd touched a nerve. She somehow had the power to make him feel bad. To hurt.

He'd never slept with a woman he didn't like in some fashion, although it was true there were a few he hadn't gotten to know any better than he'd gotten to know Darby before they'd left scorch marks on the bed. But only a few. The groupie thing had gotten boring surprisingly quickly in the early days. He still liked having someone he could talk to, at least a little bit.

It wasn't as if he didn't care about the women he'd had sex with. He'd always made sure they had a good time, too; always treated them with respect afterwards; always made sure they could get wherever they were going safely. But beyond that, as long as they cared that he'd done those things, he hadn't given a thought to what they felt about him afterwards.

Somehow, for some reason, Darby had gotten under his skin.

For some reason, he wanted her to want to stay, to see him again. He wanted her to…like him for him.

"If it makes you feel any better," she said, "I vetted you very carefully."

"That doesn't make me feel better *at all*."

There was a rumble outside. The plow. He wanted to run outside, make them go away. (They might, in fact, if a naked man ran out into the snow yelling at them.) He needed more time…

Darby stood, yanked on his pants and T-shirt. He couldn't bring himself to point out that they were his clothes. They'd be more comfortable than her dress, and they were just clothes. He didn't care about clothes.

He cared about her.

He…he was falling in love with her.

Was that even possible? After such a short time?

He hadn't felt this way with Katerina, he realized.

"Darby, wait." He reached out a hand, but didn't touch her. Not without her coming to him.

She stepped around him, her head down. If he wasn't mistaken, she might have been crying.

She pulled on her boots, her coat. She stood at the window where she'd stood that first night—only last night, although it felt like a million glorious years ago—watching the plow come into view.

Then she turned back to him. She'd blinked back her tears, but her nose was red. Pale skin like hers never lied.

"I'm sorry, Jack," she said. "I wanted to have a wonderful night with you—I wanted it to be wonderful for both of us. It *was* wonderful to me, and everything after that, even if everything after wasn't in my plan. I hope..." Her voice broke on the last word, and she swallowed hard. Tried again, as the Range Rover pulled up in the space the plow had cleared. "I hope you can remember it for the wonderful time it was."

Then she turned and opened the door.

The three-foot-high wall of snow was there, but the Range Rover chauffeur was already out of the vehicle, shoveling a path to her.

Jack realized he was naked. He didn't care, other than the fact that the open door was allowing cold air into the chalet, but he didn't want to upset the chauffeur. He looked around, saw a discarded white robe, and pulled it on.

It was the one she'd been wearing. He knew immediately by the scent of her permeating the fabric.

It was all he could do to keep his face impassive as she walked out of his life.

chapter ten

THREE WEEKS LATER, Darby accepted she was a mess.

Her work had suffered, although Jennifer had taken up the slack with grace and aplomb. It wasn't as if they hadn't done that for each other in the past, but it still made Darby feel bad.

It made her feel worse when Jennifer, the one person who knew about her list, who knew and never judged and even supported it with a certain amount of vicarious glee, *yelled* at her about it. As if Darby was a child who didn't know her own mind.

If she hadn't been so miserable, she would've gotten angry and fired Jennifer's ass. And then she'd have been without a business partner, a best friend, *and* a...a...a whatever Jack could have been for her.

Boyfriend. Lover. Maybe more.

She was on the treadmill in her gym in her house in Portola, outside of San Jose, a ridiculously overpriced Spanish Mission-style house with stucco and bright tile. She'd bought it for the land in the back, really, where she'd built her private offices. Mostly she and Jennifer worked there, although other employees at the satellite office in San Jose commuted in when needed.

She pushed the treadmill speed a point faster. Apparently she was trying to outrun her emotions. At this rate, she was going to be able to run the San Francisco marathon in a week. (Not that the marathon was scheduled in a week. Semantics.)

A TV-sized computer screen on the wall in front of her treadmill displayed the news and other information she had set up in an online feed. She was pretending to pay attention to work. She could, even, lose herself in computer neepery for minutes, even a quarter hour at a time.

The other reason she wouldn't fire Jennifer was that Jennifer was right. She *was* an idiot, she was pretty sure of it.

Jennifer had told her, years ago, that she'd created the list because she was bored. At the time, she hadn't cared. But now, with a big gaping emotional hole in her gut, she was taking a hard look at her life.

She didn't like what she saw.

Work was no longer a mountain she was moving towards. She'd arrived at that mountain, and even scaled it. There were no more challenges there, at least, not ones she was interested in.

Of *course* that was why she'd created the list.

Problem was, the list no longer looked like a fun mountain to climb.

She'd lost all interest in getting any closer to the mountain.

She'd walked away from Jack because the idea of staying with him meant she couldn't complete the list. In fact, the very idea had sent her into a panic. Now she couldn't care about the list at all. And she was sure she'd lost Jack.

She wasn't at all surprised he hadn't tried to track her down. She'd wounded his pride. She'd hurt him. She was no better than Katarina in his mind.

Stop. Thinking. About. Jack. She matched the words to her running speed until they became a mantra, until they became sounds, not words.

Two problems with that: One, they didn't work, and Two, Jack's name had just popped up on her news feed. Apparently she hadn't taken him off since checking him off the list.

She was running too fast to hit the right buttons on her tablet, so his picture and the words were right there, right in front of her, and she had to read.

In a surprise move, Jack Scandal and Scandalize booked some last-minute studio time and recorded a single, which drops just in time for Valentine's Day. Rolling Stone *reporter Tanya Booker was invited to sit in on the session, and she confirms Jack is back.*

"Jack sang every note—no auto tune, no assistance. Let me tell you, his voice sounds better than ever. 'In the Shadows' might just put Scandalize on the next Grammy ballot."

Darby groped at her tablet, but her sweaty hands fumbled it and she dropped it on the floor. The article linked to a music site, and the song started.

You make a list
For every kiss
Your eyes fixed on the prize…

Darby gasped, pressed a hand to her mouth.

It was the song he'd noodled with at the chalet, when he'd tried to explain to her what music meant.

She managed to stab at the speed button on the treadmill until it stopped, because she wasn't sure her legs would let her continue moving, much less standing.

Jack was singing about being in the shadow of a mountain, unseen.

Darby ran out of the exercise room on shaky legs. She found her phone, and on the way to the bathroom, called her assistant and told him to book her on the first flight to LAX.

Then she broke another rule.

She used her skills to find Jack's home address.

chapter eleven

IN THE END, she didn't need the information. While she was on the plane, a source contacted her with an update.

She wired the source a nice chunk of money, and by the time she got off the plane, she had a town car waiting to take her to a small club in Hollywood, and she was on the list to get in to a very important party.

chapter twelve

THE TINY BAR was jam-packed, and Jack clutched his Speyburn to keep from spilling it every time someone jostled him. Wooden tables for four fought for space with all the people milling about. The low stage itself had been barely big enough for the band and their equipment, but they'd pulled it off.

They'd pulled it off, and that, at least, felt like heaven.

The place had more of a tiki bar theme than seemed right for a rock show—more Jimmy Buffet than Scandalize—but it was the best their manager had been able to do on short notice, and Jack couldn't really complain. The acoustics had been good, and that was what mattered.

Now, though, the acoustics meant the place was loud with voices, and the air was thick with body odor and the too-strong perfume of the woman who'd latched onto him.

The bar was made of bamboo, with green fronds draping from the top. The dark wood floor-to-ceiling poles around the room were carved with tiki masks, and one wall was covered with an enormous painting of a volcano.

The woman clinging to Jack's arm said her name was Natasha, but he wasn't sure he believed her. It sounded fake. The breasts pressed against his side were clearly fake, but she really liked doing it. She was cooing about how brilliant his new song was, but she was using words like "awesome" and "sick" and "soooo," which meant she wasn't really talking about the *song*.

Across the room, Benjy—who was holding a huge, half-empty tropical drink complete with paper umbrella—pointed at him in a "You go, bro" gesture.

Jack did want to go. Away.

The private concert had been a huge success. Selected media, suits from the label, even a few fans who'd been around since the beginning, the ones who'd been on their street team in the early days.

It was the first time he'd performed live since the disastrous charity benefit show, and he had to admit he'd been nervous. Him. Jack Scandal. Not quite stage fright, but for the first time in a long, long time—not since the earliest days of the band—he'd been keenly aware of the eyes on him. Judging him. Expecting him to screw up. He'd had to shake that off, and when he did, he'd rocked the damn house.

A five-song set list that had had everyone on their feet, even during the new release.

Now, however, the performance high had worn off; he was tired, sweaty, and wanted to go home. Despite how unappealing home was.

Shake a few more hands, accept a few more praises, and then he could go. Maybe take a long drive over Mulholland, up PCH. The moon was three-quarters full and would look stunning over the ocean, and—and that reminded him of Darby, and her moon-on-the-snow comment.

He didn't want to think about her.

She was all he could think about.

He'd thought getting over Katarina was hard. Even combined with dealing with the lip-syncing fallout, that pain had been nothing compared to this.

After conferring with the band, he'd asked their manager to book them some gigs. Surprise ones in smaller venues. Get the fans excited again while they planned a bigger tour. He just wanted to perform, because when he was performing, he could turn off his brain and—

"Bro, she's here."

Benjy was at his side. His drink was now three-quarters empty. "What? Who?"

"The redhead from my birthday party," Benjy said. "The one you left with. The one you've been pining over ever since."

He hadn't realized Benjy had even noticed. He hadn't given his friend enough credit.

Then he fully processed what Benjy was saying, and he looked across the room in the direction Benjy indicated with his drink, and he saw her.

Somehow, in a room full of the elitely gorgeous, she still managed to stand out.

She was wearing an emerald green dress, sequined. Not the same one as the one she'd worn the night they met—he knew that because she'd left it in the chalet, and he'd thrown it in one of his suitcases, for no reason he could explain, along with her black silk bra and panties.

They were still in the suitcase, shoved in the back of a closet, but he knew they were there. Knew if he opened the suitcase, her scent would flow out like cartoon aroma and wind its way up his nose and wrap itself around his brain stem.

Probably not a bad way to go.

Now, even though she was on the other side of the room, he imagined her scent. And his betraying cock twitched.

He'd tracked down as much information as he could find about her. Knew the name of her company, where the offices were, where she liked to dine in the city. But he hadn't done a damn thing with any of it.

Because if she didn't want him—if he was just a name to be crossed off a list—he wasn't going to beg to be added on to the bottom for another go 'round.

He couldn't settle for that. It wouldn't be enough.

But now (he wasn't hallucinating; nobody had spiked his drink, he was sure), she was here.

She looked over at him, and smiled.

It wasn't as confident a smile as it had been that first night, but seeing her smile made his heart constrict, same as if she'd shoved her fist into his chest and squeezed.

He wasn't letting her out of his sight this time. He excused himself from Natasha, who promptly latched onto Benjy, and moved through the crowd.

Darby moved towards him.

They met in the middle.

Before he could say anything, she held up her hands. The emerald bracelet matching her earrings caught in the light.

"Before you say anything, I need to tell you something important," she said. "I threw out that list. Their loss, really. You were right: I was heading towards the wrong mountain. I have a new list now."

She took a deep breath.

He waited, not breathing, as if she'd stolen his breath from him. He just waited. And hopes.

"It's a list of men I want to kiss."

He tried to sound casual, but knew he was failing. She wouldn't be telling him this unless… "Am I on this list?" he asked.

"Yes, you ridiculous man. You're the only one. You're the only kiss on my list."

He let out a breath he hadn't realized he'd been holding. One he'd been holding since he saw her across the room. No, since she left the chalet and, he'd thought, his life.

"In the mood for a walk?" she asked.

"Absolutely not," he said. "I'm taking you home, and I'm going to make love to you in every way possible on every surface possible. Some of them twice."

"The position or the surface?" she purred, her grey-green eyes glinting with amusement.

"Either. Both."

"I've got a counter-proposal," she said.

If it didn't involve sex—soon—he wasn't sure he wanted to hear it. But he was willing to compromise, and as long as it involved *her*…

"I have a room at a very nice hotel across the street. Let's start there."

"Damn, woman, you really do want that walk."

The laughter burst out of her, unexpected and delighted, and he resolved to make that happen as much as possible for the rest of her life.

"It's not a stroll in the Alpine moonlight, but it'll do," she said finally. "Because what I really want to do is you."

chapter thirteen

DARBY HAD TROUBLE defining how she felt as she pre-
ceded Jack into the hotel room, which was decorated in
creams and golds with black lacquer accents. Not her style,
but it had been across the street from the bar and it had a
big bed.

She could've survived without the bed, even. The floor
could work just fine. Or the shower. Or...

She wanted him, yes. Again. Still.

Arousal she knew, and understood.

This other feeling, though... It was like the excitement
she felt when she made her first contact with a name on her
list: the tango, the escalation, the ratcheting up of interest
and desire.

But they were past that point—had been past it for
awhile—and this felt different. A new level of exhilaration,
of anticipation, that she felt in her belly and...she pressed a
hand to her chest...in her heart.

She didn't have time to ponder it. All thoughts fled when Jack kissed her.

He cradled her head in his large, capable hands, thumbs stroking her jaw as he tasted her. It was like their first kiss, unhurried, but less of an exploration and more of a savoring. She'd missed him so much, missed his touch so much, that three weeks apart felt like a hundred years.

She hadn't forgotten how it felt to kiss him, but now memories, details, flooded her senses. His tongue stroked against hers, and she wanted to kiss him forever, but her body clamored to feel that tongue elsewhere. As if knowing what she needed, he trailed kisses across her face, down her neck, nipping at the taut cords, soothing with his tongue.

She pressed against him, felt his erection against her stomach. Her arms wrapped around his back, she moved her hips in a slow, sensual dance, heard his breath hiss, warm against her collarbone.

"What you do to me..." he murmured, pulling back to gaze at her. He reached around her, found the zipper of her dress, drew it down. She bit her lip, not out of coyness, but because if she didn't, she might beg him to go faster.

Finally she could shrug out of the straps, push the dress down so it pooled at her feet. He took a half-step back, his eyes drinking in her body, clad only in bra and panties, navy-blue flowered lace over sheer cream, and heels. His nostrils flared.

She took advantage of the space between them to tug his shirt, a plain black sleeveless tee, out of the waistband of his black jeans and over his head. She couldn't hold back a hum of pleasure as she splayed her hands across his warm, muscled chest, feeling the tickle of hair beneath her palms. She skimmed over his nipples, and heard his intake of breath.

Good to know. She bent her head, ran her tongue across where her hand had been, tasting salt, breathing in the male musk unique to him. A scent she could drown in, a scent that sent a sharp wave of desire straight between her legs.

He muttered something that sounded like "Fecking hell" and "Jesus, woman." She reached down, curled her fingers around the long, rock-hard bulge in his jeans, felt his cock pulse even through the fabric.

With a growl, he pulled her up, yanked her close, kissed her so soundly that it stole her breath away. He nudged her backwards and she went willingly, and like the first time, when the backs of her knees hit the bed, she sat. By that point, her legs weren't going to hold her up much longer anyway.

She scooted back and he knelt on the bed, stalking her like a big cat, and her clit trembled, needy, her body remembering what it felt like to have his hands and lips on her, in her, coaxing and stroking her to orgasm.

He suckled her hard nipples through her bra, dancing his fingers between her legs—her panties already soaked—and she moaned and panted and arched into his touch. He was learning her body all over again, taking his time, ramping up her desire and need.

"So beautiful," he said. "So responsive." His teeth bit down, gently but firmly, on one nipple, and she reached down and pulled her panties to one side, offering him clear access.

He chuckled, slid one long finger into her wetness, then, frustratingly, drew it back out, tasted her. "So sweet," he added. "I can't wait to be inside you."

"Don't wait," she said. "I need you, too."

He stood, divested himself of jeans and black briefs. He paused, glanced around, and spotted the bowl of condoms on the night table. A laugh rolled out of him. "Feeling optimistic, were we?" he asked as he reached for one.

"I have confidence in our abilities. Would you have expected anything different?"

He caught her hand in his, fingers twined with hers. "No," he said simply. "Not from you."

As he ripped the packet open, she couldn't resist wrapping her fingers around the steely length of his cock and swipe a thumb through the moisture glistening at the tip. Watching him, she licked her thumb. A promise for later. She couldn't imagine ever getting tired of that.

Her fingers shook a little—from need, not nerves, she told herself—as she helped him slide the condom down.

Before he entered her, as her legs wrapped around him, he

He thrust into her with long, steady strokes that coaxed a slow-building, inexorable orgasm from her, one that pulsed through her in long, delicious waves of pleasure.

He pulled her up, settled her on his lap, cock buried deep inside her, and kissed her. A moment later, they found their rhythm together, rocked together, ramped up together until their kisses grew erratic.

"Darby," he gasped, and she moaned "Jack," and this time her climax gripped her like a vise, and when she came, it was her arms around him and his arms around her that kept her from flying apart.

Sometime later—they had all the time in the world now—sipping Speyburn, curled together, naked, he said, "I kept imagining this, but I never thought it would happen. At first, I hoped you might reconsider, that you might call…"

"I thought about it." She swirled the caramel-colored whiskey in her glass. "But I didn't think you wanted me to. After all, you didn't call either."

He pressed his lips to the crown of her head. "You'd made it pretty clear I'd already been crossed off your list."

"I don't play with people's hearts, Jack," she said quietly. "The list was a game, I suppose, but it was never meant to hurt anyone. And if one person on the list didn't work out, I had backup plans. I didn't have a backup plan for you. I don't have any backup plan now." Admitting that sent a wave of fear through her, like a wash of ice water. But then…the fear was gone.

He'd said, *If you don't let go and let the music take you, you'll never find the heart of it.* That was even more true of love.

"What changed your mind?" he asked.

"The song. 'In the Shadows.' I heard it, and I realized…I realized I might still have a chance. That you might forgive me."

"There was nothing to forgive," he said, easing away so he could see her face. His eyes were fathomless pools of deep blue. "You never lied to me; you never promised anything more than one night. I didn't come after you because I respected your choice." A smile played on his lips. "After all, mountains can't move."

She couldn't stop the answering smile that curved her mouth. "I had to come to the mountain, on that detour that was really the right path after all."

"So now what?" he asked. "I assume you have a plan?"

"Not a clue," she said. "There's this whole perfectly useless afternoon thing I'm trying out."

She felt his chest move as he chuckled. "Good for you. How about, room service, foreplay on the sofa over there, sex in the shower, a nap, more room service…"

"Goodness, you've given this some thought."

"I'm also hoping for a freak snowstorm."

She laughed. "I don't think you're going to get that wish."

"I'll settle for the rest of it." He took her chin in his fingers, tilted her head so he could lay a long, smooth kiss on her that took her breath away. "All I know is, I'm not letting you walk away this time."

She thought her heart was going to crack open. Now she needed him to hold on to it for her, keep it safe.

Just as she would keep his safe.

"I don't need to," she said. "Remember, the only kiss on my list is yours."

And she pulled him down for another one.

"Legendary erotica heavy-hitter" –Violet Blue

ANDREA DALE

Brava
Novella Contest
TOP TEN
FINALIST

She yearned
to hold him…

in her
HANDS

Turn the page for a sneak preview of
In Her Hands, the first novella in the
scintillating With Her Heart trilogy.

chapter one

SARABETH LICKED HER lips in anticipation as she gazed at the male perfection that awaited her.

She slipped an Evanescence CD into the stereo and cranked the volume. The pulse-pounding beat wasn't the only thing that made her hips twitch as she walked to where he stood.

Waiting for her.

She was in complete control. It was a heady, empowering feeling. She could touch him in any way she wanted.

But she teased herself, putting off the first contact. Instead she walked slowly around him. She'd molded each faint bump of his spine already, cupped her hands around those taut cheeks. Teased the dimples that cut into his hips. Traced the juncture where buttocks met thigh.

She walked back around to face him. God, he was beautiful. Her hands trembled, ever so slightly, when she reached up and rested them on his firm chest. Smooth, and faintly cool. He would heat up soon enough under her touch.

Sarabeth dipped her hands in the bowl of water and raised them again. She trailed her fingers along the ridges of muscle, outlining them, defining them. Nipples bloomed to life beneath her fingertips. She circled the hard nubs, fingernails tweaking ever so gently. Her breath hissed between her teeth.

Oh, yes.

A drop of water trailed down, hesitating at the crease of his thigh, and she longed to follow it with her tongue. She licked her lips again, and flicked the droplet away from the crisp hair with her thumb.

Teasingly, she tickled his belly button, smoothing her fingertip around the indentation. Beneath it, a treasure trail of hair pointed down. But she wasn't ready to go there yet.

Not just yet…

Another douse in the water, and her hands slipped along his narrow waist, resting briefly on the sharp hipbones. He had a birthmark on his left hip. She touched the crescent moon shape like a blind woman reading Braille, sensitive skin sending distinct signals to her brain.

Erotic signals.

Was it getting hot in the room? She felt sweat trickle down her own back, but she was too intent on the body before her to stop and open a window.

She outlined the six-pack muscles of his abdomen, her own stomach fluttering at the touch. She longed to have him touch her in the same way, to feel his strong hands caress her flesh.

Evanescence's lead singer wailed about her immortal.

He was her immortal, Sarabeth thought. He consumed her senses. But right now, she was the one with the power.

Now.

Now was the time to touch him, really touch him. Touch him for the first time. She'd been waiting so long. Her hands trembled again, from anticipation and the barest frisson of fear. So long she'd waited. Another moment, and there would be no going back. Some women could, but she couldn't. Once she started, she was committed, all the way to completion.

She pressed against the hard muscles in his thighs, closed her eyes, imagined. Then she dipped her hands in the water again and closed them around his manhood.

She coaxed, gently at first and then with more assurance, bringing him to life between her palms. Long, firm. Not too thick. She wrapped her fingers around him, analyzing the circumference. Stroking his length from end to tip, she marveled at how perfectly he fit in her grasp.

She pressed her thumbs along the smooth ridge of his proud head, shaping the smooth mushroom cap. The veins beneath caught her attention, and the ridge just below the head. She caught her tongue in her teeth as she worked her ministrations.

Leaning in so close that she could smell him, she cupped the twin sacs, massaging gently. But he distracted her, and she couldn't stop herself from gently stroking him again.

Her breath came in shorter gasps as she neared completion.

God, he *was* perfect.

Sarabeth stepped back and beheld her creation, what she had brought to life with her own hands.

She glanced out the window at the billboard that stretched across the building opposite: an advertisement for Noir for Him cologne. The model regarded her with eyes filled with sensual promised. He was shirtless, his jeans unbuttoned just far enough and the bulge below outlined just enough to tantalize the imagination of any straight woman between sixteen and, well, dead.

Her eyes flicked between the billboard and the clay torso on the pedestal in the middle of her studio. She'd didn't think she'd taken too much artistic license by making him nude—and hard.

***

Michael was early for his date with Jill. The mâitre d' took him to a table in the brick courtyard, which was framed by palms that shaded the diners from the sun but still allowed some peeking by the rabble on the street.

It was just the type of place Jill would choose. Just the type of place Michael preferred to avoid like the proverbial plague.

He didn't have to wait long in the dappled Los Angeles sunshine before Jill arrived. He rose as she approached the table. The statuesque redhead turned her head slightly, allowing him to kiss her cheek while at the same time showing her best profile to any fans on the street, any paparazzi with cameras she hoped would be trained on them.

He felt her coolness. He knew before his butt hit the chair again that they were over.

"You do understand, don't you?" Jill laid a hand over his. Intimate, but not too intimate.

"I do," he said. He waited for sadness to come, perhaps even anger to sting, but all he felt was a small hint of regret.

He'd met Jill when his face, if not his name, was already a household feature (it was the jeans ad spread in *Esquire* that had done it, paired with the beer commercial during the Superbowl that had more women watching football than ever before) and she had been a rising star.

Now he was still a household feature, but her first movie (in which she'd played the ingénue sidekick) had fired the public's interest, and her second, which she'd just finished filming, had everyone abuzz.

Jill toyed with her salad fork. Most of the salad remained in her dish. He'd tucked into his grilled ahi without a problem—a guy still had to eat. The teriyaki-wasabi sauce had been exquisite.

"We had some good times, didn't we," she asked, her smile fond.

"We did," he agreed. "Next you're probably going to say that you hope we can be friends, and—" he held up a hand to forestall her "—the answer is, yes, we can."

He'd known, all along and deep down, that at least part of what attracted her to him was that on his arm, she would be noticed. At his side, her career had the chance to bloom. Despite that, towards the beginning of their relationship he'd thought that they might have had a chance at something bigger.

The sex had been great. They'd had a fine rapport out of bed, sharing a taste in movies (even if she'd dragged him to every premiere in the hopes of camera time), imported beer, and antique glass.

But her latest movie shoot had been on location in Prague for nine months, and every time he'd offered to visit, the timing had never been right for her. He'd started to wonder...

Lunch over. Relationship over. Their goodbye kiss was on par with a handshake ending a business transaction.

No sadness. Just regret, and a level of weariness, like a heavy comforter threatening to smother him.

Was it too much to ask for a woman who wanted him for *him*, not what his celebrity status could do for her? Someone who could see beyond the hunky male model?

He walked Jill to her new, cherry red Jag, then left the parking garage alone.

Ah well. It left him with the afternoon free to go for a run on the beach before he getting ready to meet Brad for another art gallery opening that his friend was dragging him to.

***

"Well, how do I look?"

Sarabeth danced out from behind the carved teak screen that separated her bedroom area from the living area of her loft. She posed, preening, one hip thrust forward to accentuate her leg.

"Like you're going to bring men to their knees tonight," her best friend, Anya, said. "Damn, you're hot enough to turn a straight woman."

The corset top, purple satin covered with black lace, molded to Sarabeth's figure, while the attached short, flippy, purple chiffon skirt showed off her legs to great advantage and hinted at the lace tops of her black thigh high stockings.

"Oh, as if you're not wearing your prowling outfit," Sarabeth retorted. Her friend had gone the Goth-punk-schoolgirl route, with a short, pleated plaid skirt, fishnets, and boots; perversely, she smelled of White Shoulders.

But Anya was already, as usual, distracted, disappearing into Sarabeth's studio space.

"I want to see the latest—the one you said had you all hot and bothered," Anya's voice came through from behind the white sheets that hung to bisect the loft.

"I'm not quite ready to show it to anybo—"

Anya screamed in delighted horror.

"—show it to anybody, but I take it you've already found it." Sarabeth pushed aside the drapes and found Anya in front of the sculpture.

"Oh my God oh my God! I can't believe you *did* that!"

Sarabeth grinned. "Yeah, well, it was kind of an afterthought."

"*That* could never be an afterthought." Anya ran to the window and stared out at the billboard lit against the darkness, then came back to where Sarabeth and the lifelike sculpture stood. The statue was just the torso, but if Sarabeth had given it a head—the head atop the neck, that is—they would have been staring into each other's eyes.

Lustfully.

"It's your best yet," Anya said. "Are you really going to show it? I mean, it really looks like him. The birthmark is a dead giveaway."

Sarabeth blinked herself out of her reverie. At this rate, she was going to have to change her thong before they left for the gallery opening.

How many times had she made herself come while staring at his image, while imagining his touch? She treated her videotape of his beer commercial like a porn flick.

Fantasies could be dangerous, but she'd thought this one was safe enough. Until all of her work started looking like him.

Until this piece, where she'd taken it farther than ever before.

"I don't know," she said, finally answering Anya's question. "I know I'm pushing it with the birthmark. I could cover it up, I suppose."

She didn't want to. She wanted to press her lips to the curved moon, and feel the tremble of hot flesh.

Anya's hand hovered over the statue's erection.

"No touching. It's not dry," Sarabeth warned.

"When it's dry, could I touch it, oh pretty please? I could put this to good use."

"What if it broke?" Sarabeth asked reasonably.

"Dildo!" Anya shouted, spinning around in a giddy circle.

Sarabeth's brain clicked off as she imagined a dildo shaped like her fantasy man.

Yep. Definitely time to go change that thong.

***

"She really dumped you?" Brad looked appropriately sympathetic. "Sheez, if she'll dump someone like you, I don't stand a chance."

"Nope," Michael said. "You don't have nearly enough Hollywood clout for her."

The art gallery was Brad's baby; he handled the displays and special shows while a semi-silent partner dealt with the money matters. Brad's tastes tended towards classical art, but he still allowed for a variety of styles, just to be fair.

The gallery was in a former Hollywood hotel, retaining much of its Art Deco décor. The grand lobby—now the main exhibit space—had etched glass and terrazzo floors, and graceful arched metal women flanking the fireplace. Ferns hung in gilt baskets; light jazz filtered from hidden speakers.

To go with the theme, Brad favored a white waistcoat and black bowtie. It somehow worked with his close-cropped blond hair and grey eyes.

"It's because you told her you want to quit, isn't it?" Brad asked.

"I never told her that."

Brad was, in fact, the only person that Michael had told. When you'd been friends from someone since childhood, you had that kind of rapport. He'd never really had the chance to tell Jill, anyway. Which said something right there about their relationship.

It wasn't as if he wanted to completely quit modeling. It wasn't awful, and the money was, in fact, incredible. He liked that a lot. But more and more, he wanted to be behind the camera.

He knew his photographs were good. Brad had been bugging him to do a display at the gallery, but he wasn't ready for that yet. He didn't want to feel that he'd gotten the showing because his friend co-owned the place. He'd do it when it felt right and he felt ready.

"You can do both, you know," Brad said. "Look at Viggo Mortensen—you know, that Aragon guy."

"Aragorn."

"Whatever. Apparently he also paints, writes poetry, yadda yadda. A real medieval man."

"Renaissance man."

"Whatever."

"I suppose." Michael snagged a flute of champagne from a passing waiter's tray and sipped it. Good stuff, he thought appreciatively. "People already took him seriously as an actor, though. It's different with me. They tend to assume I don't have a brain in my pretty little head."

"Most guys don't have brains in their *little* heads." Brad snorted into his champagne. "Sorry. I know you're being serious. So prove 'em wrong—show them you've got an MBA *and* artistic talent to boot."

"I'm thinking of doing it under my real name. At least that would be one good thing to come out of the pseudonym." Michael hated that he'd naively caved in to his agent's pressure and taken on a "stage name." She swore it would ruin his career if he changed back to his own name. He wasn't sure he believed her, but he knew the transition would be tricky.

"And then, when you're famous for the photography, you can come out," Brad continued. "Well, not like that, but you know what I mean. Use both names, like John Cougar Mellencamp did."

"Brad," Michael said carefully, "what's my public name?"

"Michael Steele."

"And what's my real name?"

"Michael Barr."

"And what happens if you put them together like John Cougar Mellencamp?"

"Michael Steele Ba… Oh." Brad pressed his lips together, obviously trying not to laugh.

Michael shook his head and took another sip of champagne.

And nearly choked when he saw her.

He'd thought he'd been sexually attracted to Jill. Compared to his reaction to the woman across the room, his feelings for Jill had been as if he'd been a Puritan. And she'd been his Puritan sister.

His mystery woman—and, amazingly, he already thought of her as "his"—had a certain resemblance to Catherine

Zeta-Jones in "Chicago": similar black bobbed hair, just a little longer; ripe, dark, kissable lips; sultry eyes that, even though they hadn't turned in his direction, were enough to pierce through him. But he would walk right by Ms. Zeta-Jones (whom he'd met once, at a party, and who had been positively delightful) for the woman across the room.

The top of her dress harkened back to the Victorian era, but there was nothing prudish about how the corset, with its satin-and-lace straps, hugged her waist and pressed her breasts upward like a creamy offering.

Michael wanted to pour champagne down her cleavage and then rescue every drop with his tongue. In the fantasy, he could hear her gasp with pleasure, could taste the mixture of champagne and flesh, could envision her tossing her head back in abandoned ecstasy.

At this rate, Michael thought, easing behind a sculpture of twisted metal, he was going to have to pour the champagne down his own crotch to relieve his sudden, aching erection before he got thrown out of the art gallery for indecency.

Unfortunately, that thought led to the fantasy of the woman drinking the champagne off his cock, and *that* was no help at all in relieving the erotic pressure in his pants.

"Are you okay, man?" Brad asked.

Michael started to answer, but his response came out as a strangled gasp. He cleared his throat and tried again.

"Just admiring that woman over there."

Brad followed his gaze. "Oh yeah, her. Isn't she a cutie? I think she's in a band. God, I love that schoolgirl-punk look."

"Not her, her friend."

"Oh. She's hot, yeah, but she's…I dunno, tall. And I've heard she's kind of…"

"What?" Michael's stomach dropped. She was a lesbian. Brad was going to say that she was a lesbian. Damn.

"Uh, creative. Inventive," Brad said.

Michael's hopes soared again. "Meaning?"

"She's not averse to…variations. Kinks, maybe."

His brain flashed more images: The woman in leather. The woman with her hands bound, writhing beneath him and begging for release. The woman in front of a large window at night, daring somebody anonymous to watch. The woman…

It wasn't really anything he'd spent a lot of time thinking about until now. He'd had partners with whom he'd played the naughty-librarian game, the I've-been-a-bad-girl game. The games had been fun, but they'd been games.

Now he was thinking about it. Just standing over there, she made him think about it.

He hailed a waiter and exchanged his empty glass for a full one.

"How in the world do you know that?" he asked Brad.

His friend grinned. "She's an artist, and it's my job to know about artists. In fact, she's doing the next show here. Her friend, the blond, is on our mailing list. You going to go talk to her?"

"The blond?"

"No, bonehead, the tall one. The one that has your knickers in a twist."

The woman in question turned suddenly, causing her sassy purple skirt—a well-placed contrast to the corset—to flare out. Michael caught a glimpse of lace at her thigh.

His mouth went dry.

"In a minute. I need an opening line."

"'I'm a world-famous male model' isn't good enough for you? How about, 'I've got an amazingly big d—'"

"Why don't you use that one on the blond?" Michael suggested.

He stared across the room. Around him, conversation ebbed and flowed. It was a coup for the artist that someone of his stature attended the gallery opening, but really, he couldn't find it in himself to care about the art, or even the artist, right now.

He wanted her.

As he watched, she plucked a cream puff from a tray and popped it into her mouth, slowly sliding her fingers back out between pursed lips to catch any crumb. Her eyes closed in an expression of sheer carnal delight.

Would she look like that when her lips were wrapped around his cock? Would her eyes close helplessly when he entered her, or would she stare at him, pupils dark and dilated with passion?

Her tongue flicked out to secure any remaining cream.

She turned, and saw him.

Her tongue remained poised on her lower lip, inviting, glistening.

A long moment. Michael forgot what breathing was like. His vision narrowed. Sound faded.

And then she smiled.

***

Sarabeth was reasonably sure that someone had slipped a hallucinogen into the utterly divine cream puff she'd just eaten.

That couldn't be him over there, not really.

He was staring at her with so much…hunger. Her nipples hardened, pressing almost painfully against the satin of her corset. Just from the look he was giving her. Never in her wildest fantasies had she imagined him fixing such a predatory look on her.

Her wildest fantasies promptly got more detailed and wild.

If this was a hallucination, then she might as well run with it.

Just to make sure, she smiled at him.

She saw his nostrils flare as he sucked in air. Oh, he'd seen her, all right. No hallucination.

"Holy crap on a stick," Anya said.

Sarabeth jumped. She'd practically forgotten Anya was standing next to her. Hell, she'd pretty much forgotten what her own name was.

"That's him, isn't it?" Anya hissed.

"I believe so, yes," Sarabeth said, not taking her eyes off him.

"Jesus, he looks just as good with his shirt *on*," Anya said appreciatively.

Sarabeth had to agree. He wore a royal blue button-down shirt that she suspected might be silk. Oh, she wanted to find out if it was silk. Wanted to run her fingers along the front of it. Wanted to peel it slowly off of him and suggest he run it along her naked body.

Then she could put her hands on his chest for real. Not cold clay, but hot, yielding flesh.

She stifled a moan.

"What are you going to do?" Anya asked.

Anya probably knew exactly what she was thinking, but if she spoke it out loud, her friend would never let her live it down.

"I'm going to…"

She had been about to say that she was going to go talk to him, but the decision has been taken away from her. He was heading straight for her.

He wore black pants that fit him oh, so very well. His thighs pressed against the material as he walked. She wanted to feel those hard muscles trapped between her legs as she rode him to completion…

Anya said something about not being a voyeur and darted away, leaving Sarabeth standing alone.

This is what a wounded gazelle must feel like when the lion's stalking her. Trapped. Bracing herself to be devoured.

The thought of his teeth scraping against her skin made her legs tremble.

Then he was right in front of her, so close she could smell his strong, masculine scent.

"I'm not the artist," she said. At his confused look, she continued, "I saw you looking at me, and thought you must have assumed I'm the artist." She indicated the sculpture display. "I didn't do these."

"Do you know the artist?" he asked.

His voice was like melted chocolate dribbled down her spine in anticipation of his tongue licking it all back off.

She shook her head. "No, I've never met him."

"So, what do you think of his artwork?"

She tore her gaze away from him and glanced around at the twisted lumps of metal.

"I think," she said carefully, "that it's not so much art as scraps leftover from high school shop class. Not so much art as…leftovers. If that's what he was going for, then I'm afraid he lost me in the process."

"Oh, thank goodness," he said. "I was hoping it was just me." He held out his hand. "Michael Barr."

Too many sensations. The warmth of his flesh, the firmness of his grasp—oh, where she wanted him to grasp her, and caress her!—the tingling sensation on her palm as he drew away and his fingertips trailed across her nerve-heightened skin.

Your love slave, she thought, but thankfully she managed to answer aloud correctly. "Sarabeth Delaney."

"And you're an artist, Sarabeth?"

His voice lingered over her name as if tasting it. Savoring it. She wanted to hear him say it, husky with passion, as she tasted him in turn, pressing her lips against salty….

"I'm a sculptor," she said. "And you?"

"Photographer."

Did she sense the slightest hint of hesitation before he answered? And, she mused, he'd introduced himself with a different last name.

He probably didn't want to be recognized, she decided. That was common enough in Hollywood. Stars were people, first and foremost, and an evening was far more enjoyable if they could have normal conversations and not be fawned over.

Fair enough. If that's the way he wanted it, that's exactly how she'd handle it. He didn't need to know she was already obsessed with him.

As long as she didn't give herself away by tearing off his clothes and jumping him in the middle of the gallery. Because lord knew her hands were trembling to do exactly that.

"Have I seen any of your work?" he asked.

Oh honey, just wait 'til I have you naked and I'll show you my work. "My first big show is the next one on the schedule here. In two weeks."

His eyes, blue pools she wanted to luxuriate in, showed appreciation. "That's wonderful. You must be very excited."

He couldn't know how excited. How her entire body craved another sample of his touch. How if he touched her between her legs, he'd find her hot and wet and on the edge of explosion.

What turned her on the most was that he obviously wanted her, too. She could see it in the darkness of his eyes, in the way his nostrils flared again when she took a sip of champagne, and in crotch.

She tried very, very hard not to stare at the obvious thickness pressing against his trousers.

She had to clench her hand into a fist just to keep herself from reaching out and touching…

He dipped his head close to hers, and when he spoke, she could feel his breath tickling her ear, an erotic, warm breeze. She stifled a moan.

"So, Sarabeth Delaney the Sculptor," he murmured, "why don't you show me the rest of the gallery and tell me what you think of the art?"

To give herself time to get her legs to find the strength to move, she toyed with the choker at her neck. She was gratified to see his eyes drop to her cleavage, and linger there.

He, too, seemed to be struggling for control.

What an aphrodisiac *that* was.

She'd never been one for one-night stands, for anonymous sex. Despite her long-standing lust for this man whom she'd never met prior to the last ten minutes, she didn't know anything about him. He could be…dangerous.

Oh, she already knew that he was dangerous. She'd had no idea that she'd react to him so completely, so totally, upon being in his presence.

That she would be willing to throw all caution to the wind just for the chance to be closer to him. To press against him. To feel him.

Rational thought fled. All she knew was that she wanted him, and he wanted her.

She could cope with dangerous, she decided. It would be worth it in the end.

For now, though, it did make sense to get to talk with him more in a public place. Get to know him as a person. See how riled up she could get him, with the flirting and the teasing. How much she could get him to want her. To need her.

But, God, the things she wanted to do to him.

She wondered how long she could hold out. How long before she broke down and excused herself to the ladies room where she could relieve the aching need that threatened to consume her?

"I'd love to," she said.

***

Michael dragged his gaze from her cleavage and his mind away from the fantasies regarding her cleavage, and struggled to remember what he'd just asked her that she was so willingly agreeing to. *Please, let it be something good.*

Then she was hooking a hand through his arm and leading him into the next room, out of the rotating gallery collection and into one of the permanent displays. The motion restarted the blood flow to his brain enough so that he recalled they were going to look at more art.

He didn't want to look at art; he wanted to look at *her*.

But he was willing, for a while at least, to settle for being with her.

Her light touch on his arm sent his senses tingling. Her fingers rubbed the silk of his shirt against his flesh, a maddening sensation. She was close enough that he could see the light glinting off her blue-black hair. The perfume she wore—something flowery, but not cloying—brought his cock to attention again. How could something so simple affect him so strongly?

All he knew about her was her name, and that she was a sculptor.

He didn't need another relationship right now.

Or did he? Granted, she hadn't batted an eyelash at his introduction, so maybe, just maybe, she didn't recognize him. Maybe he had a chance at developing a rapport with somebody who didn't want him for anything bigger—

Although his cock was getting bigger by the moment, and that just had to be tamped down before he hurt himself or those around him.

"Now, this piece, I like," Sarabeth said.

Michael forced himself to concentrate on her words. Not the husky timbre of her voice. Not how that voice would sound when she cried out his name in the heat of passion, as he brought her to—

Damn. Must…pay…attention.

She indicated a metal sculpture, this one in bronze. It was a stylized horse, rearing up, head thrown back in abandon.

"There's movement, even in something as solid as metal," she said. "You can feel the wildness, the pass—" she coughed, recovered "—the passion."

"As if the horse is going to leap off the pedestal," Michael said.

She turned appreciative eyes on him. "Exactly."

"This one's sad, but beautifully done." Now she stood before a painting.

Michael considered it. It showed an empty, rumpled bed. What he took to be the morning sun shot through a window at the head of the bed, a sunbeam bisecting the bed in a streak of red-gold. To either side of the bed, however, the room got darker as it extended away in either direction. Michael looked at the plaque beside the painting. It read, simply, "Separation".

"I know the artist on this one," Sarabeth said. "She did it just after she and her husband split up. The pain's there, in every stroke."

Michael looked more closely. On either side of the painting was a doorway, each shrouded in shadow. Faintly, he could see the form of a person in each doorway: on the left a man, on the right, a woman. They each were looking back over their shoulders, but it was obvious that the darkness and the gap were too overwhelming. They were already too far apart to have a hope of reconnecting.

"You're right, it is sad," he agreed. He thought, fleetingly, of Jill. He couldn't drum up a fraction of the emotion that was found in the picture. If he had loved her…well, in his way, he had. But it was gone, and the door had shut.

"I didn't mean to bring us down," Sarabeth said softly. "Let's go look at something else."

"I think I'm getting a sense of what you like in art," Michael said. "Emotion."

"Honest emotion," she agreed. "A piece of artwork can be technically perfect, but that's not enough in the end. A vase of flowers is one thing. A vase of flowers that look like they're about to flutter in a breeze, that a petal is going to drop…that they were given by a lover to apologize for a misunderstanding…"

"It takes a lot of talent to create something like that."

"It does. Talent, and—"

"Passion?"

He said it to tease her, but the word caught on his lips as it had on hers.

"Oh hell."

He wasn't sure which one of them swore.

He was pretty sure they both lunged at each other simultaneously, meeting midway in a searing kiss.

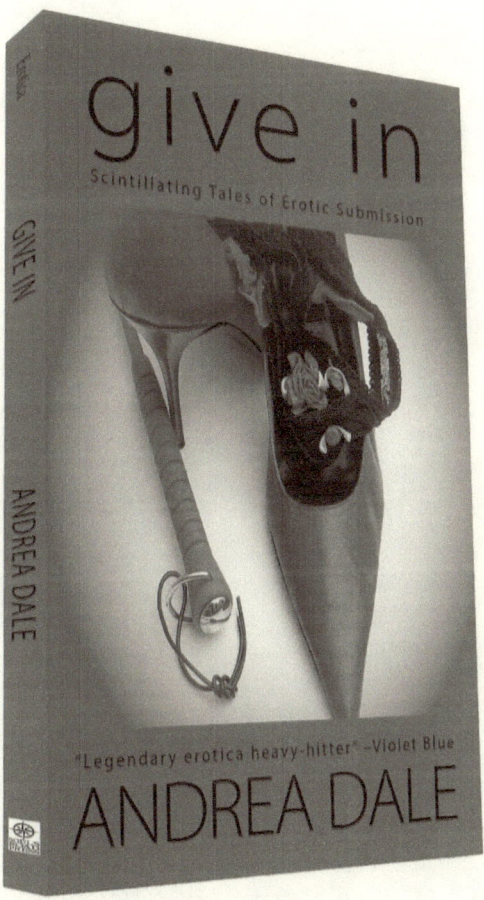

about the author

Called a "legendary erotica heavy-hitter" (by the über-legendary Violet Blue), Andrea Dale writes sizzling erotica with a generous dash of romance. Her work—which has been called "poignantly erotic," "heartbreaking," and "exceptional"—has appeared in fourteen year's best volumes as well as about a hundred other anthologies from Soul's Road Press, Harlequin Spice, and Cleis Press, including her recent novella, *Kiss on Her List*.

She finds passion in rock music, clever words, piercing blue eyes, the wind in her hair, and the scent of the ocean.

Visit AndreaDaleAuthor.com for more information.